Tales of the Plumed Serpent

Tales of the Plumed Serpent

Aztec, Inca and Mayan Myths

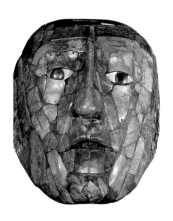

DIANA FERGUSON

Photographs by Mireille Vautier, Paris

COLLINS & BROWN

First published in Great Britain in 2000 by
Collins & Brown Limited
London House
Great Eastern Wharf
Parkgate Road
London SW11 4NQ

Distributed in the United States and Canada by Sterling Publishing Co,
387 Park Avenue South, New York, NY 10016, USA

A CIP catalogue record of this book is available from the British Library.

ISBN 1 85585 823 1 (hardback)
ISBN 1 85585 862 2 (paperback)

1 3 5 7 9 8 6 4 2

Editorial Director: Sarah Hoggett
Project Editor: Katie Hardwicke
Editor: Liz Cowen
Designer: Claire Graham
Illustrations: Mireille Vautier
Map Artwork: Julian Baker

Colour reproduction by Bluetag Ltd, London
Printed by Imago Ltd, Singapore

Illustrated Library.com
Visit *Illustrated Library* where you can view thousands of books and images,
compiled from some of the world's finest publishing houses, all on one site.
http://www.illustratedlibrary.com

CONTENTS

LANDSCAPE OF THE MYTHS

VENEZUELA

COLOMBIA

Quito ▲

ECUADOR

BRAZIL

Cajamarca ▲

Moche ▲

PERU

Lima ▲
Pachacamac ▲

Machu Pichu ▲

Cuzco ▲

BOLIVIA

Nazca ▲   *Lake Titicaca*   ▲ Tiahuanaco

PARAGUAY

CHILE

ARGENTINA

Approximate
boundary of the ——
Inca Empire

Santiago ▲

MEXICO

TOLTECS
▲ Tula
▲ Teotihuacan
▲
Mexico City/
Tenochtilan
AZTECS

GULF OF
MEXICO

YUCATAN
▲ Chichen Itzá
Mayapán ▲
Uxmal ▲

MIXTECS
Monté Alban ▲
▲ Mitla
▲ Oaxaca
ZAPOTECS

OLMEC

TABASCO

MAYA
LOWLANDS

Palenque ▲

▲ Tikal

Yaxchilan ▲

—— BELIZE

MAYA HIGHLANDS

GUATEMALA

▲ Copan

HONDURAS

EL SALVADOR ———

NICARAGUA

PACIFIC OCEAN

COSTA RICA ———

PANAMA ——

INTRODUCTION

WHEN THE SPANISH SET FOOT on the soil of the New World in the sixteenth
century, they stumbled upon civilizations completely unknown to them
which had been flourishing independently of any outside influence and
rivalled those of the Old World. They found vast cities with huge stone monuments as
impressive as the ancient pyramids of Egypt; they saw empires and systems of social
and political organization as ordered and complex as any across the Atlantic; they
encountered alien gods and witnessed religious blood rites, impenetrable and barbaric
to the European mind; and, best of all, they found riches which they could not have
conjured in their wildest imaginings, an Aladdin's hoard of precious stones and silver
and, most prized of all, gold – golden jewellery and statuary and religious icons, even
whole rooms lined with the precious yellow metal.

And yet the people who were the creators and masters of all these marvels had
neither the wheel nor iron tools and were – technically – living in the Stone Age.

This was the world which opened up before the amazed eyes of the Spanish
adventurers. It is also the world of the myths and folktales in this book, which offer a
peephole into the religious beliefs and cultures of the indigenous peoples of Mexico
and Peru and their near neighbours.

THE LAND BETWEEN
THE WATERS

Although archaeologists and other
researchers are always making new
discoveries which alter our perceptions
and knowledge of peoples of the past, it
is currently believed that the inhabitants of
both the Americas were part of the great wave
of immigrants who – perhaps as much as 50,000
years ago – crossed the 'ice bridge' over the Bering
Strait which linked Siberia with Alaska before the

end of the Ice Age. They are all now called Native Americans or 'Indians' – an erroneous title which arose because Christopher Columbus, not knowing that there was a western land mass between Europe and the East, took the New World for the Indies (India and the Far East) when he arrived there in 1492.

Some of these migrants settled in North America; others continued south, into Anahuac – the 'Land Between the Waters' – the ribbon of land which connects the continents of North and South America and is flanked by the Caribbean Sea to the east and the Pacific Ocean in the west. Anahuac is the ancient name for Mexico, a country which is part of the region known as Mesoamerica. As well as eastern and southern Mexico, Mesoamerica takes in the Yucatán peninsula, Belize and Guatemala, and extends down into Honduras and El Salvador.

The ancient peoples of Mesoamerica include the Olmecs, Zapotecs, Maya, Toltecs, Mixtecs and Aztecs. Although they spoke different languages and flourished at different periods in history, what we know about the Mesoamericans reveals that they were culturally united in many ways. They shared a 260-day calendar, for example; they played a particular type of ritual ballgame; they had gods in common, although perhaps under different names; and they believed in the giving of blood and human life to propitiate the gods.

EARLY MESOAMERICANS: OLMECS, ZAPOTECS AND MAYA

Of these peoples, the Olmecs developed the earliest known Mesoamerican civilization. They first appeared in lowland Veracruz and Tabasco around 1200 BCE (BCE: before Christian or common era. CE: Christian or common era) – at about the same time as Tutankhamen's reign in Egypt. Although they remain an enigma, we do know that the Olmecs built cities and used a complex system of inscribed signs and symbols – as yet undeciphered – which represented their gods and religious symbols. They also carved jade, produced ceramics and had a sophisticated artistic style which was later to influence other Mesoamerican cultures.

Most notable among their artistic achievements are the colossal and finely chiselled portrait heads which they carved, with stone tools, from blocks of stone weighing up to 16,300 kilograms (36,000 lb) each, some of which were transported more than 80 kilometres (50 miles) to their resting places. By 400 BCE Olmec culture had died out.

By 600 BCE, if not before, another very ancient civilization had arisen in the highlands of Oaxaca – that of the Zapotecs. The Zapotecs are believed to have invented the first Mesoamerican system of writing and probably also its first calendar, as well as having knowledge of astronomy. From their capital Monte Albán they dominated the region, recording the dates of their victories and depicting their captives on large stone slabs, in carvings entitled 'Los Danzantes' – literally 'the dancers'. Monte Albán was their capital for more than a thousand years and, at its peak, had a population of about 25,000 people. The Zapotecs also established the city of Mitla. Although their power declined eventually, Zapotec culture still survives in Oaxaca.

In the second century BCE, on the high plateau of central Mexico, the seeds of another civilization took root. Here a tribe of primitive farmers began to extend the temple mound in their village and slowly built it up into a gigantic monument, which became the Pyramid of the Sun. They added a wide avenue which ran from this monument to another, the Pyramid of the Moon, and to a courtyard sacred to the rain god Tlaloc, and the Plumed Serpent, the god of the wind. The pyramids dominated the landscape and the village around them grew into the city of Teotihuacan, the 'Place of Those Who Became Gods'. We do not know the ethnic identity of its inhabitants, so they have simply been named after the city they built – they were the Teotihuacanos. At its peak, the city covered 21 square kilometres (8 square miles) and may have been home to 200,000 people. Teotihuacan flourished until about 650 CE. The Teotihuacanos traded with the Maya, who adopted some of their practices, especially their war cult. Later, the Aztecs also drew on Teotihuacan, taking its two pyramids as the site of a key episode in their mythology – the creation of the Fifth Sun.

Further south, in southern Mesoamerica, the cultural development of the Maya began at about the same time as the rise of Teotihuacan. This was in what is known as the Late Preclassic period (300 BCE–200 CE); the golden age of the Maya, however, came in the Classic period (200–900 CE), when their civilization was centred in the lowland rainforests of northern Guatemala. They were skilled builders, accomplished sculptors, painters and potters, sophisticated astronomers and inventive

mathematicians – they are believed to have been the first people to use the concept of 'zero'. Perhaps most importantly, they were pioneering scribes, for it is Maya writing which sets them apart from other Mesoamerican peoples.

The script which they developed was a combination of logographs (word pictures – for example, the logograph for *balam*, jaguar, was a jaguar's head); symbols representing phonetic syllables, such as 'ba' or 'la'; and semantic symbols that specified which of several meanings was intended. The invention of this syllabic writing was unique in the Americas and its diversity allowed great subtleties to be conveyed. Such an invention facilitates a breadth of communication, not only across space but also through time. It would have allowed Maya speakers in different locations to recognize shared beliefs and culture; also, by recording events, it preserved an account of Maya history that could be passed on to future generations.

However, the competition between the various Maya city states, under the rulership of different kings, was greater than the unifying power of any script, and the Maya did not come together in a single, coherent empire under one ruler. Contrary to the romantic image so long held, these were not a peaceful people. Instead, the various cities – such as Tikal, Copán, Yaxchilan and Bonampark – lived in conflict with each other.

In the end, Classic Maya civilization imploded upon itself. Rapidly expanding populations and the inefficient and intensive farming methods used to meet the growing demand for food, as well as continuing warfare, may all have contributed to its collapse. By 900 CE, the golden age of Maya civilization had ended. Many of the Classic sites were abandoned as the Maya moved out of lowland Guatemala and spread south and north into other areas, including the lowlands of Yucatán. Here they continued to live until they were conquered by the Spanish in the mid-1500s.

Today, more than two million people, living in Mexico, Guatemala, Honduras and Belize, are their descendants. They speak over thirty different Maya languages and are the inheritors of traditions and religious beliefs going back centuries.

LATE MESOAMERICANS: TOLTECS, MIXTECS AND AZTECS

At around the same time as Classic Maya civilization was declining, another power was rising in the highlands of central Mexico – that of the Toltecs. At Tula, about 70 kilometres (45 miles) north of Mexico City, the Toltecs built their capital city; later Aztec legend tells of a fabled city called 'Tollan', which archaeologists have identified with Tula. From the tenth to twelfth centuries, the Toltecs maintained an empire and dominated most of Mexico.

Myth and history are blended in what we know of this group. Tula was ruled by a succession of nine kings, each of whom was accorded the divine title 'Quetzalcoatl', the same as that of the Plumed Serpent god, signifying their godlike status. In central Mexican myth, the god Quetzalcoatl is expelled from his royal city, Tollan, and moves to the 'red lands' in the east, most probably Yucatán. Here, the ruins of the important Maya city of Chichen Itzá show a strong Toltec influence, and may have been built by Toltecs using forced Maya labour. The Toltecs were great traders who travelled far afield, and Tula and Chichen Itzá certainly shared a special relationship during the Early Postclassic period (900–1200 CE).

South of the Toltec heartland, in the Mexican states of Oaxaca, Puebla and Guerrero, the Mixtecs rose to power in about 900 CE. Speaking a language similar to that of the neighbouring Zapotecs, they were an artistic people who produced fine

works in gold, jewellery and painting. Politically, they remained a loose confederation of kingdoms. They did, however, have one brief period of glory when, under their great warrior leader Eight Deer Ocelot Claw, they defeated the Zapotecs and conquered Monte Albán and Mitla.

Later, in the fifteenth century, both the Zapotecs and Mixtecs were subjugated by the Aztecs; the men of three whole Mixtec tribes lost their lives as sacrificial victims in the dedications of the great temple in Tenochtitlán, the Aztec capital.

The Aztecs were the creators of the last Mesoamerican civilization before the arrival of the Spanish. Calling themselves the Culhua-Mexica, they were among the nomadic invaders from the north who crossed the frontiers of the Toltec empire in the twelfth century. Like the Toltecs and others, they spoke Nahuatl. Since the nineteenth century these Culhua-Mexica have been grouped with other Nahuatl-speakers under the name Aztecs after Aztlan, the place from which legend says they came. They gave their name to the country in which they settled: Mexico.

According to their mythology, these Culhua-Mexica, or Aztecs, were nomads for many years, seeking a 'promised land'. They finally found it at a swampy site in the Valley of Mexico, where they built their capital city, Tenochtítlan, now Mexico City, in 1345. In the two centuries which followed, they replaced the Toltecs as the most powerful race in the region, and established the greatest empire Mesoamerica has ever seen.

Part of the Aztecs' imperial style included adopting some of the gods of the people they had conquered and imposing their own gods in return, especially the sacrifice-hungry Huitzilopochtli, their solar god. They even had a temple, the Coateocalli, in which they imprisoned idols of alien gods whom they wished to demote. This policy of absorb-and-conquer was useful. Claiming the gods of the region as their own legitimized the Aztec presence, and the religious cohesion which they imposed both consolidated their position as rulers and provided cultural unity.

The Aztecs were economically successful, exacting heavy taxes in the form of goods from their subjects and travelling far afield in the pursuit of trade. Of all the Mesoamerican peoples, they are also the most closely associated with the practice of human sacrifice. The thousands of victims whose living hearts they offered to their gods were often culled from the populations of subject peoples. The taxes they extorted and the human sacrifices caused much resentment and later led some subject groups to forge alliances with the Spanish.

And yet the Aztecs, who were on the one hand warlike imperialists, were also capable of producing great beauty. When the Spanish first saw Tenochtítlan, they were dazzled by it. It had a population of between 200,000 and 300,000, more than any contemporary European city. Canals were the island-city's roads, along which boatmen plied their canoes. Aqueducts supplied it with fresh water and causeways connected it with the lake shore. There were gardens, a zoo with exotic animals and a thriving market. In the ceremonial precinct stood the Hueteocalli or Templo Mayor, whose southern shrine was dedicated to Huitzilopochtli and northern one to the rain god, Tlaloc – and all of this came under the rule of the Great Speaker, as Aztec emperors were known.

The Spanish arrived in 1519. Two years later, in 1521, they had accomplished their mission and the Aztec empire was at an end.

THE INCAS

Further to the south and later, in the early 1400s, another and perhaps even more extraordinary empire grew, ruled by the Incas. The level of political and social organization which held this vast territory together is reminiscent of that of the Romans. Centred on its capital city, Cuzco, the empire stretched for more than 4020 kilometres (2500 miles) along the western edge of South America and included parts of what are now known as Colombia, Ecuador, Peru, Bolivia, Chile and Argentina.

Correctly the 'Inca', or Sapa Inca, is the term applied to the supreme monarch, but the name came to describe all members of the dynastic, ruling élite to which he belonged. Originally the Incas were a tribe, or group of tribes, living around Cuzco. They began to grow in power in the early thirteenth century, but it was not until 1438, when the ninth Inca, Pachacuti, defeated an invasion by their neighbours the Chancas that the empire as such really began. Pachucuti went on to conquer other regions, and Inca expansion and unification was continued by his son, Topa Inca Yupanqui, and grandson, Huayna Capac.

The Incas called their empire Tahuantinsuyu, the Four United Quarters. Keeping the Quarters together demanded skilled administration and tight social control. Inca rule can be seen in two ways: as a despotic order which depended on forced labour and the appropriation of resources by the state; or as a paternalistic system which ensured for its obedient peasant subjects freedom from hunger, military attack and theft.

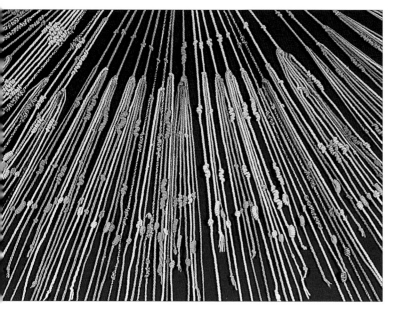

The Incas spoke Quechua, but surprisingly never developed a system of writing like those of Mesoamerica. Instead they used a device called the *quipu*, a cord with knotted strings of different colours and lengths, to record statistical information and – in some way still unknown to us – Inca mythology and history. Trained *quipucamayoqs*, or 'knot-keepers', used and read the *quipu*.

The Inca empire, already weakened by civil war, fell to the Spanish in 1532.

THE CHRONICLERS

What we know of the mythology of Mesoamerica and the Incas comes from several sources. These include painted ceramics and stone carvings, illuminated manuscripts produced by the indigenous peoples themselves, and written accounts collected in colonial times by Spanish chroniclers.

The illuminated manuscripts from Central Mexico and Maya territory take the form of screenfold books – long, folded scrolls of bark paper or deerskin – which are known as *codices* (*codex* in the singular). The brightly painted scenes on them show gods, mythological events, rituals and other cultural information, and often relate to cycles or periods in the sacred calendar. Since most of the indigenous sacred books and writings were destroyed by the Spanish as 'idolatries', only twenty-five of the codices are known to have survived, eighteen of which are painted in pure, pre-Hispanic style.

One sacred book which bridges the gap between these hieroglyphic records and modern texts is the *Popul Vuh*, or 'council book'. When the Spanish arrived in Mesoamerica, they wanted to convert the indigenous peoples to Christianity but, in order to do so, they first needed to understand native culture and religion. There were no historical documents to help them, however – at least, not in any written form that they could understand – so they developed a spelling system, in the roman script of Europe, to record native languages. In the sixteenth century a Maya nobleman used this system to transcribe what must have been a hieroglyphic manuscript into written Quiché, the Maya language of highland Guatemala. The original was lost but later, between 1701 and 1703, a Quiché-speaking Dominican priest, Fray Francisco Ximénez, found the transcription, copied it, and translated it into Spanish, thus making it accessible to all Europeans.

The *Popul Vuh* is the most important single source we have of Maya mythology. It presents it in a broad sweep, telling of the creation of the world, of the exploits of two pairs of hero twins and, finally, of the founding of the Quiché dynasties. The middle section, dealing with the hero twins, is the most ancient: images of this part of the narrative are found in Maya art as early as the Late Preclassic (300 BCE–200 CE).

Like the Quiché transcriber of the *Popul Vuh*, the Maya of Yucatán also wrote down their traditions in the newly devised spelling system. The most important of these documents is a set of books named after Chilam Balam, a Maya priest and prophet who foretold the coming of the Spanish. Although none of these works was written before the eighteenth century, they refer to ancient mythology and probably drew on old screenfold books.

The Aztecs also produced written accounts in Nahuatl, their language. The *Leyenda de los Soles* may have originated in this way. Probably taken from one or more pre-Hispanic documents, this tells – in formal and archaic Nahuatl – of the creation of the world, humans and maize, of the god Quetzalcoatl at Tollan, and of Aztec history.

But the most comprehensive account we have of Aztec culture and mythology does not come from the pen of a native Nahuatl-speaker, but from that of a Spanish priest – Bernardino de Sahagún, who arrived in Mexico in 1529. More tolerant of the native people than others among his countrymen, he produced his *Historia General de las Cosas de Nueva España*, based on information gleaned from the sons and grandsons of the Aztec nobility. This massive work consisted of twelve volumes with over 1850 illustrations. When it was realized that full conversion of the natives to Christianity was not being achieved and that many were reverting to their old beliefs, Sahagún's work was suppressed. A copy of it resurfaced in 1779; it is now housed in the Laurentian Library in Florence and is known as the Florentine Codex.

Another Franciscan priest, Fray Andrés de Olmos, was the author of *Historia de los Mexicanos por sus Pinturas*, an important account of Aztec creation mythology, while over in Yucatán, the Franciscan Fray Diego de Landa wrote his *Relación de las Cosas de Yucatán*, which covers the history, rituals and calendrical beliefs of the Maya of that region.

Since the Incas made no written records of their history or mythology, we have to rely even more heavily on the Spanish chroniclers for what we know of Inca culture and religion. In reading these documents, we must remember that the Spanish were not unbiased and often presented the Inca ruling class as tyrants in order to justify their own role as conquerors.

One of the earliest Spanish chroniclers was Cieza de León, a soldier who came to Peru in 1547. He travelled extensively, talking to the native peoples, and recorded what he learnt in his *Crónica del Peru*, published in 1553 and 1554. Another chronicler, Juan de Betanzos, who had married the daughter of the Inca ruler Atahaulpa and was fluent in Quechua, was ordered by the viceroy of Peru to produce a history of the Incas. He completed it in 1557, under the title *Suma y Narracion de los Incas*.

Francisco de Toledo, who was Peruvian viceroy from 1569 to 1581, ordered further investigations into Inca history, including the political structure of the empire. Like the Spanish priests in Mesoamerica, Toledo needed, as it were, to know his enemy before he could completely reorganize the colony as he wanted. *Quipucamayoqs* and

members of the former Inca nobility were interviewed and among the resulting reports were Pedro Sarmiento de Gamboa's *Historia de los Incas*, completed in 1572, and Cusqueñan Cristobal de Molina's *Las Fabulas y Ritos de los Incas* of 1575.

Two other chronicles are worth noting. The first is Garcilaso de la Vega's *Comentarios Reales de los Incas* of 1609–17. De la Vega was the son of an Inca princess and a *conquistador*, and wrote his history, which contains numerous myths, in Spain. The other work, which appeared at around the same time as the publication of the first part of the *Comentarios*, was a manuscript written in Quechua. In English translation, it is known as *The Huarochirí Manuscript*. Apparently produced under the direction of Francisco de Avila, the local priest, it deals with the mythology of one of the provinces in the former Inca empire, the Huarochirí area in Peru's central highlands.

Today, at the beginning of a new millennium, we no longer view the mythologies of the Maya, Aztecs and Incas as the Spanish priests often did, as diseases which they needed to understand in order to cure. Sadly, however, in attempting to learn more about these once-great peoples, all we have to work with is what we have inherited – cultural jigsaw puzzles in which many of the pieces have been lost, either through deliberate destruction or simple lack of preservation.

And yet spiritual beliefs as powerful as those involved here cannot be totally extinguished. Like half-conscious streams of memory they will continue to flow in the imaginations and outlook of those who are genetically descended from the vanished pyramid-builders, star-gazers and empire-makers – those who still speak the old languages such as Nahuatl or Quiché or Quechua. Perhaps, like the ancestors of the Maya, the gods are still there, invisible in water and thunder and air. Or perhaps, like the mythic Inkarrí of the Andes who lies underground, they are not dead, but sleeping.

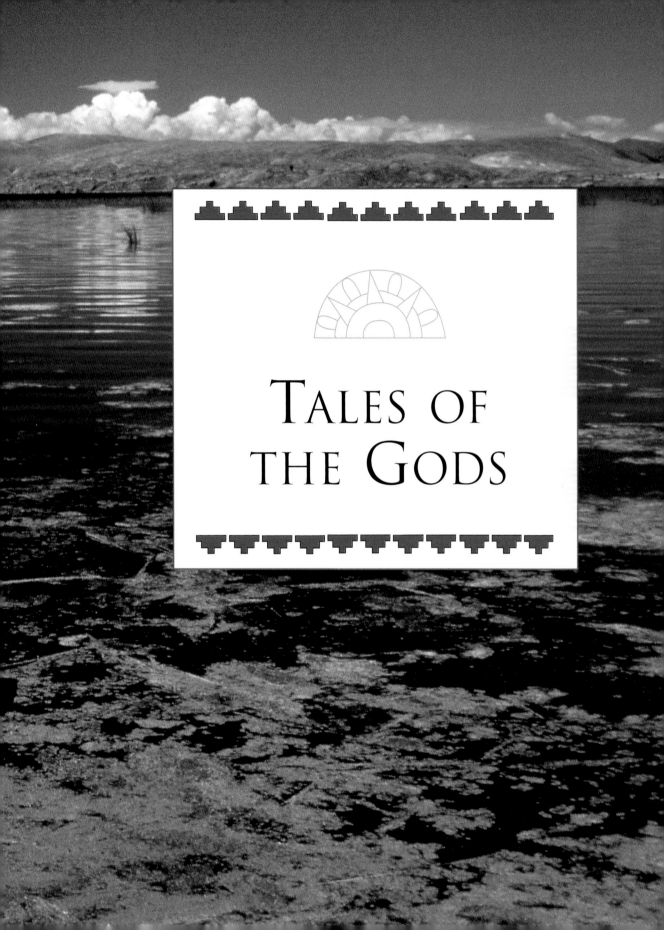

TALES OF
THE GODS

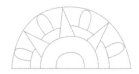

THE SELECTION OF MYTHS in this chapter shows how the peoples of Mesoamerica and the old Inca empire explained how the world was made. Some of their themes are universal, others have a particularly Amerindian flavour.

Like all creator gods, the deities here exist outside the bounds of time and physical reality; they simply are. They inhabit primordial waters – Lake Titicaca or the Maya 'lake-sea'; they infuse the heavens with their presence; or they are immeasurably ancient and are called Grandfather and Grandmother. Their initial creations are not always a success. Hurricane and Plumed Serpent, the Maya gods, try three times to make the human race out of that quintessentially Amerindian plant – maize – before they succeed. The Andean Viracocha also makes a race of giants, whom he turns to stone, before making humans out of clay. Petrification is a favourite trick, but it is not unique to these gods; nor is the idea of the existence of an earlier giant race. Viracocha's giants evoke the Greek Titans, the Norse giants and the Fomoire of the Irish Celts.

In the story of Pachacamac, the metaphor of crop growth from a dismembered body is found in myths and folktales around the world and has an agricultural basis: in order for a crop to grow, you must first 'bury' it – plant it in the soil.

Several features give these stories a particularly local flavour. First, the Mesoamerican gods do not furnish the world fully before setting humans in it, as in other mythologies: these humans have to wait in darkness for the rising of the Sun. Second, both 'The Four Suns' and 'Pachacuti' reveal the strong Mesoamerican and Inca tradition of cycles of creation and destruction, in which each age is known as a Sun. In 'The Four Suns', this destruction is caused by the opposition between the 'dark' Tezcatlipoca and the 'light' Quetzalcoatl, a dualism which runs through Aztec myth. And finally, in 'How the Gods Made the Sky-Earth', the new world is envisaged as a field to be tilled and cultivated. Creation itself is seen as the act of sowing seeds, and is equated with dawning.

HOW VIRACOCHA CREATED LIFE

• INCA •

I N THE BEGINNING there was only darkness. In the heart of darkness the land lay sleeping. And in the middle of the land, like a slice of obsidian nestling in the Earth's navel, lay Lake Titicaca.

Slowly something in the depths of the lake stirred. The waters rippled and churned and out of the foaming eddies a figure rose. He placed one foot, then the other, on the land and looked about him. He was Con Ticci Viracocha Pachayachacic, the Maker, the Dweller in the Void, the Teacher of the World, and he had come to bring life to the Earth.

Viracocha began the work of creation. So that the Earth would no longer be empty he made a race of giants to inhabit it. But all did not turn out as the Teacher of the World had wished, for it was not long before all the creatures he had made angered him so much that he was forced to turn them to stone. For good measure, he also sent a great flood called *unu pachacuti*, the water that overcomes the land, to drown everything that he had made.

Again Viracocha began on the work of creation. Raising his voice, he called out the Sun, the Moon and Stars from where they were sleeping on the Island of the Sun on Lake Titicaca. To each he gave its place in the heavens, and its time. But when the Sun saw the Moon he was jealous, for the Moon's face was brighter than his own. So he took a handful of ashes and threw it at his rival to dim his brilliance. That is why, to this day, the Moon has a cloudy face.

Viracocha continued with the work of creation. Bending down by the shores of Lake Titicaca, he scooped up clay and squeezed and pummelled and pressed it until he had moulded, out of the raw earth, the first men and women, and he painted them according to the styles of dress they would wear, from all the different nations. At the same time he made all the animals and the birds, allocating to each one the place where it should live and the food it should eat and giving each bird its song.

But it was not yet the clay people's time to live, so Viracocha sent them back into the Earth, from where they had come, into the caves and springs and mountains, there to await the call to life. Thus did the Maker sow the seeds of the ancestors, whose children would inhabit Tahuantinsuyu, the land of the four united quarters.

There were two clay people, however, who did not return to the Earth with the others. Viracocha kept them with him to help in the work of creation. Their names were Imaymana Viracocha and Tocapo Viracocha.

The three Viracochas set out north-westwards from Lake Titicaca. Imaymana Viracocha went between the forests and the mountains. Tocapo Viracocha went by the sea. Con Ticci Viracocha Pachayachacic took the path between them, which leads through the highlands.

As they walked their separate ways, they called to the people waiting in the Earth and named the nations to which they belonged. And at their command the people came out, blinking, into the light.

As they walked, they named the trees and the plants and told them when to flower and when to bear fruit.

As he walked on his path between mountains and sea, the Maker came to a place called Cacha.

Here the people, who had already come out of the Earth, did not know their creator and began to attack him. But Viracocha went down on his knees before them, raised his arms skywards and called down fire from heaven. The people were terrified and begged for forgiveness, whereupon the god touched the flames with his staff and they died down, but not before they had scorched the land and sucked all the substance from

STONE AGE BUILDERS

The towering pyramids and rich carvings of ancient Mesoamerica and the austere edifices of the Incas are all the more extraordinary because they were constructed by peoples who had neither iron tools nor the wheel. Their tools were mostly made from stone, flint and obsidian. As for the wheel, it seems to have been unknown, perhaps because there were no strong draught animals such as horses or oxen to pull wheeled vehicles.

Given these limitations, the architectural and engineering feats of the Incas, in particular, are astonishing. They were skilled road-builders – roads being essential to effective rule of their empire. Inca roads, like Roman ones, were straight and tunnelling through or climbing over physical obstacles, such as mountains, rather than skirting around them. On the plains, they were wide enough, according to the Spanish, to accommodate eight horsemen riding abreast. In hot areas, canals alongside provided water and trees were planted for shade. In the desert, where sand threatened to obscure a road's course, marker posts were erected as a guide. Around 16,000 kilometres (10,000 miles) of road made up the total network.

Inca architecture is even more impressive, though little is known about the exact techniques employed. No mortar was used to glue together the huge stone slabs that form the walls – cut and shaped, it is believed, with tools made of harder stone; the walls stand because the slabs interlock so perfectly. For added strength, buildings and door and window openings were given a trapezoid shape, with inward-sloping vertical sides, to displace weight downwards. So strong were they that, when earthquakes rocked Cuzco, colonial buildings tumbled but the stones in the Inca walls simply 'bounced' and settled back in place again.

Without wheels, wagons or draught animals, the beasts of burden were men – 30,000 are said to have been involved in the construction of the fortress of Sacsayhauman at the Inca capital of Cuzco. Built of stones weighing up to 125 tons (17,000 kilograms) each, the fortress lies on a river that was once diverted through a system of stone conduits to give the city its water supply. In the countryside irrigation canals covered vast distances, running across aqueducts over gorges and in tunnels through mountains.

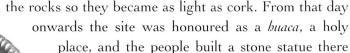

the rocks so they became as light as cork. From that day onwards the site was honoured as a *huaca*, a holy place, and the people built a stone statue there and made it offerings of gold and silver.

As he walked, on his path between mountains and sea, the Maker came to the place that would be called Urcos. Climbing the peak which rose before him, he seated himself and called forth the people sleeping in the mountaintop. Later, in memory of this moment, their descendants would set a golden bench on the peak and place on it an image of the god, which they called Atun-Viracocha.

As he walked on his path between mountains and sea, the Maker came at last to the valley where the shining city of Cuzco would one day rise. Here he called forth from the Earth a great lord whom he named Alcavicça, which was also the name of the people who came to live in the valley. But before leaving, Viracocha gave one final instruction. After he had gone, he commanded, another race must rise from its soil – the Incas, rulers of the empire of Tahuantinsuyu.

Having completed his work, the Maker continued his journey north-west until finally, by the ocean's shore, in the land that white men call Ecuador, he met once more his two sons, Imaymana Viracocha and Tocapo Viracocha. Without breaking the rhythm of their gait, without varying their pace, the three Viracochas set their feet on the ocean's broad and rolling highway and walked on, pushing westward over water and wave, wave and water, until at last they vanished from sight, like the Sun in the evening when it plunges into the sea.

> *You who are without equal, and span the ends of the earth:*
> *you who gave life and force to human beings,*
> *saying to one, 'Let this be a man',*
> *and to the other, 'Let this be a woman',*
> *you gave them being: let them live without danger, in peace and health.*
> *You who are in the heavens and in the thunderstorm,*
> *grant them long life, and accept this our sacrifice.*

Inca prayer to Viracocha

26

PACHACAMAC, THE SON OF THE SUN

• INCA •

BEFORE THERE WERE people to breathe the air and walk the wandering pathways of the world, there were Pachamama and Pachacamac. Pachacamac was the son of the Sun. Pachamama was Mother Earth and the soil, stones and mountains were the substance and shape of her body.

Pachacamac looked about him at the silent and empty world. 'I will fill it with life,' he thought. So he made a man and a woman and went away satisfied, thinking that he had done enough. But what he had forgotten – or did not yet know – was that living things need more than the breath of life to live. They need food to sustain them and Pachacamac had created none.

The man and the woman grubbed about in the soil and searched under the stones, but nowhere could they find anything to feed their hollow bellies and hunger gnawed at their insides. In the end, it was too much for the man and he died.

Fearing the same fate for herself, the woman prayed to the Sun. In answer, the Sun sent his life-giving rays into her womb and made a child. Four days later she gave birth to a son.

When Pachacamac saw what had happened, that now he had a brother, he was seized by unbearable jealousy. He waited until the woman wasn't looking, then he snatched the child and killed and dismembered it, burying the pieces of its mutilated body in the soil. There they lay like seeds and, in time, like seeds they sprouted, pushing their green shoots out of the Earth,

enriched and made fertile by the boy's blood. From the teeth came corn. From the bones came the white roots of the yucca. From the flesh came vegetables and fruit. Thus out of death was brought forth life, and food, the Earth's boon, was given to humankind.

But from the navel and phallus of the dead child no plants sprouted. Instead the Sun took these parts, which were the vital essence of his murdered child, and made for himself a new child, who was in every respect the same as the first. His name was Vichama. Because he was the son of the Sun, who travels the sky all day, Vichama had wanderlust bred in the marrow of his bones. He longed to travel and so soon he set off to journey the world.

In his absence, Pachacamac returned to his task of destruction, killing Vichama's mother – the woman whom he himself had made – and leaving her skeleton to be picked clean by condors and vultures.

Then he began the work of creation all over again. But this time, when he made a new man and woman, he made sure that they did not starve like the first couple had. Instead, they grew in health and strength and had many children, who in turn had more children, so that before long there were whole communities of people living in the valleys and on the hillsides. They were governed by the *curacas*, the headmen, whom Pachacamac himself had chosen.

But this orderly creation was not to last. Like the Sun, who always comes back to where he started, Vichama finally returned. Rage filled his heart when he saw what Pachacamac had done. Gathering up the remains of his mother, he arranged all the parts in their correct places. 'Come, flesh, come,' he whispered, and flesh grew once more on the bare, bleached bones, and his mother came back to life again.

Then he turned to the people whom Pachacamac had made, stirring their pots by the fire, tending their crops in the fields, sleeping in their hammocks, and he transformed every one to stone. Wherever they were, whatever they were doing, each remained transfixed on the spot, petrified for all eternity.

Finally Vichama prayed to the Sun. 'Father, send new life,' he asked.

In answer to his prayer, the Sun made three eggs. One was made of gold, one of silver and one of copper. The shell of the golden egg cracked first and out of it stepped the *curacas* and the noblemen. The shell of the silver egg cracked next and out came all the noblewomen. The shell of the copper egg cracked last and out came all the ordinary people.

Meanwhile, Pachacamac, afraid of the vengeance of Vichama, fled to the west, where, like the Sun his father, he dissolved into the ocean. Ever since then the place where he disappeared has borne his name. It is the sacred shrine of Pachacamac, which lies just south of the city of Lima. Here pilgrims in their hundreds have come to worship him and to hear the words of his sacred oracle.

As for Pachamama, whose bones and flesh are the Earth on which we all stand, she too is honoured, but in another way. To this day, the Aymara Indians of Lake Titicaca make offerings to her of potatoes stuffed with coca leaves. These they bury in the soil in tribute to her, the Mother, and in the hope that she will be generous to them in the harvest to come.

> *My Sun, the golden garden of your hair*
> *Has begun to flame*
> *And the fire has spread over our corn fields.*
>
> *Already the green ears are parched*
> *Pressed by the presence of your breath*
> *And the last drop of their sweat is wrung from them.*
>
> *Strike us with the rain of your arrows,*
> *Open to us the door of your eyes,*
> *Oh Sun, source of beneficent light.*

Quechua poem to the Sun

THE FOUR SUNS

• AZTEC •

Up in the highest of all the thirteen heavens, in Omeyocan the Place of Duality, floated Ometeotl, the mysterious, the unknowable, the two-in-one. Ometeotl was neither wholly male nor wholly female, but both encompassed in a single entity. He-and-She was Ometecuhtli and Omecihuatl, the Lord and the Lady of our Flesh.

In this coming together of opposites He-and-She gave birth to the first race of gods: Red Tezcatlipoca or Xipe Totec the Flayed One, god of the east; Blue Tezcatlipoca or Huitzilopochtli, the Hummingbird, god of the south; Quetzalcoatl the Plumed Serpent, god of the west; Black Tezcatlipoca the Smoking Mirror, god of the north; and Tlaloc, lord of rain and lightning, god of the centre. Together they made the world, the creatures on it, the sacred calendar and fire.

But soon two of the gods rose in anger against each other. In the battles that followed the pendulum of victory swung to and fro between them, as steadily as the alternating of day and night. With the defeat of one the old world was destroyed, the Sun extinguished. With the triumph of the other a new world was born and a new age dawned lit by a new Sun. Of these ages there have been four, the duration of each being mirrored with minute exactitude in the divisions and conjunctions of the sacred calendar.

But who were the two gods involved in the cosmic wars that brought the world down, who opposed each other as light opposes dark? They were Quetzalcoatl, the bright-feathered one, and his adversary Black Tezcatlipoca, owner of the sorcerer's mirror of shadows.

It was Tezcatlipoca who ruled the first Sun, which was an age of earth. The population of this world consisted of primitive earth-dwellers – huge giants with such prodigious strength that they could uproot whole trees like saplings, with nothing but their bare hands. When Quetzalcoatl set about Tezcatlipoca with his staff and defeated him by knocking him into the sea, the god of the first Sun took his world with him. Rising from the waves in the form of a mighty jaguar, he propelled himself heavenwards, where he left his footprint on the night sky in the constellation of the Great Bear. Taking this as their signal, all the jaguars on earth fell upon the giants and devoured them. When the big cats had finished their feast all that remained of the once-great race was an assortment of mammoth-sized bones. Fossilized in ancient strata, these endured, waiting to tantalize the imaginations of a future generation.

So the first Sun ended on Nahui Ocelotl, 4 Jaguar, the day after which it is named.

The second Sun, an age of air, was ruled by Quetzalcoatl in his guise as the life-giving wind who walks before Tlaloc, the rain, to clear his path. When Tezcatlipoca came to do battle with his rival and defeated him by knocking him to the ground, Quetzalcoatl took his world with him, raising such a mighty wind that it carried everything away – people, houses, even the wind god himself, who metamorphosed into his own essence. The only survivors from the age of air are their descendants, the monkeys, who still swing from the forest branches like flotsam blown there by a storm.

So the second Sun ended on Nahui Ehecatl, 4 Wind, the day after which it is named.

The third Sun, which came into being with the victory of Tezcatlipoca, was ruled by Tlaloc. It was an age of rain, but rain of an unusual sort, for it burned rather than refreshed. Rising once more from defeat, Quetzalcoatl extinguished this third Sun in a downpour of fire which blackened the sky and reduced the world to ashes. So devastating was the fiery fallout that it caused the population to mutate. Arms sprouted feathers, feet grew claws, noses became beaks: the people of the world turned into turkeys.

So the third Sun ended on Nahui Quiahuitl, 4 Rain, the day after which it is named.

The fourth Sun, which came into being with Quetzalcoatl's victory, was an age of water, ruled by Chalchiuhtlicue, Lady Precious Green, goddess of streams and still water. This world perished in a flood so massive that it washed away the mountains and brought down the sky. Unable to live underwater, the people of the world underwent a sea change: discarding bone and flesh for scale and fin, they became fish.

So the fourth Sun ended on Nahui Atl, 4 Water, the day after which it is named.

There were two, however, who escaped the fishy metamorphosis of their fellows. Tezcatlipoca – who naturally knew of the impending deluge in advance – singled out one man and his wife for salvation. Their names were Tata and Nene. Forewarned by the god, the couple took refuge in a hollow log and waited there until the flood receded. Their only food, the god said, was to be a single ear of corn each. But when at last the tide receded and the couple emerged, what first met their eyes in the shallows before them was a fish. Neither knowing nor caring that it had once been human, but thinking only of the ready meal it would provide – for raw corn kernels had long lost their appeal – the couple seized upon it. Kindling a fire, they roasted their catch and settled down to a cannibalistic feast.

The smoke from the fire rose up to the sky, where it met the sensitive nostrils of the star gods Citlallinicue and Citlallatonac. 'Who is making fire down there? Who is smoking us out?' they complained.

Tezcatlipoca knew and at once descended to earth. 'What did I tell you? What did I say? And did you obey me? No, you did not!' he raged at his protégés. And in a movement as swift and deft as that of the blade which removes a sacrificial heart, he sliced off their heads and placed them on their buttocks. The hybrids that resulted, odd and back to front, were the first dogs.

The gods looked about them at the world. The earth was flattened, the sky had collapsed. Something would have to be done. So the gods of the four directions, of north, south, east and west, got together and built four roads leading to the centre of the world, which divided it into quarters. Next they crept beneath the fallen sky and raised it, like the roof of a vast tent, above the earth-plain. Finally, Quetzalcoatl and Tezcatlipoca, whose competitiveness had caused so much destruction, began to work together. To shore up the sky and prevent it from falling again, they transformed themselves into two mighty trees, which stood braced between heaven and earth, keeping them apart. The tree of Quetzalcoatl glinted with the emerald-green feathers of the quetzal bird. The tree of Tezcatlipoca glowed with polished obsidian mirrors.

In reward for what the gods had done, Tonacatecuhtli made them lords of the heavens and unfurled before them a broad swathe of stars, which stretched across the night sky. This was the gods' highway, by which they moved to and fro. It is called the Milky Way.

There is, however, another version of events, a darker tale of a fifth world born out of violence and blood.

Tezcatlipoca and Quetzalcoatl, so the story goes, were watching the she-monster Tlaltecuhtli, moving about in the primordial sea. To accommodate her insatiable desire for flesh, she had, as well as a single cavernous maw well supplied with teeth, sprouted several other mouths, which now snapped and gnashed at the elbows, knees and other joints of her reptilian body. With such a creature in their midst, how could the gods hope to complete a new creation?

So, transforming themselves into two giant serpents, Tezcatlipoca and Quetzalcoatl seized Tlaltecuhtli. One took her left hand and her right foot, the other her right hand and her left foot and – ignoring her cries of rage and agony – they pulled and pulled till they had pulled her apart.

The gods threw half of the mutilated body up to form the sky. The other half, left floating on the sea, became the earth. The gods themselves did not emerge wholly unscathed, however, for Tlaltecuhtli bit off Tezcatlipoca's foot, which he had used as bait to lure her out. From then on, he had only one good leg and had to replace his missing foot with an obsidian mirror.

The other gods, who had seen the dismemberment of Tlaltecuhtli, came to console her. 'Hush,' they whispered, 'for on you life itself will depend.' And so it was. At the command of the gods, the earth-body of Tlaltecuhtli changed, bringing forth everything needed to sustain humankind. Her hair became the soughing trees and the sighing grasses, her skin the smaller plants. Her limpid eyes and their sockets became wells and caves, her nose hills and valleys, her shoulders mountains.

But old appetites linger and at night, from deep within her carapace of soil and rock, the goddess still howls for blood. To ensure her continuing favour, she is fed the hearts of men.

So, one way or another, this way or that, a new world was made. But there were no people to inhabit it. How should they be made? They must be created from the bones of their ancestors, the gods decided – the skeletal human remains of the fish

people of the Flood. Accordingly, Quetzalcoatl, the Plumed Serpent, descended to Mictlan, the underworld of the dead, to retrieve them.

Presiding over all of Mictlan was Mictlantecuhtli, who was the Lord of Death. His terrifying skull head swayed when he talked. His bones clattered when he walked.

'What is your purpose here?' he asked Quetzalcoatl. As the god explained his errand, wily Mictlantecuhtli saw an opportunity for some sport. He agreed to give up the bones, but in return Quetzalcoatl must perform a small task – 'A trifle, really, no more' – he must travel four times around Mictlantecuhtli, blowing a trumpet made from a conch shell.

Quetzalcoatl agreed. When the Lord of Death placed the instrument in his hands, however, he discovered that it was not a trumpet but a plain shell without holes to blow through. Undeterred, the Plumed Serpent enlisted the help of worms to eat holes in the sides of the shell and bees to make it hum with sound.

Since the god had successfully completed his task, Mictlantecuhtli at first agreed to let him take the bones. But when, soon after, he went back on his word, Quetzalcoatl made off with his booty. Quickly, the Lord of Death sent his servants ahead of the escaping god to dig a pit to entrap Quetzalcoatl. As he approached it, a quail fluttered in front of him. The Plumed Serpent was startled. He stumbled. He fell headlong into the pit and lay there senseless, as if dead. The bones which the god was carrying broke into pieces of different sizes.

When at last the Plumed Serpent revived and made good his escape from Mictlan, he took the broken bones to the sacred place called Tamoanchan, where he gave them into the hands of Cihuacoatl, the Snake Woman. She then ground them like cornmeal into a fine powder, which she poured into a pot. One by one, the gods came and pierced their bodies and allowed their blood to drip on to the bonemeal.

Blood and bone together were the basic substance from which the new race of humans was formed. But because the bones had been broken into different sizes, people, too, vary in height and girth, being tall, short or of medium height, and either fat or thin.

So the fifth world was created and the people to inhabit it, but as yet there was no new Sun to light it. How the fifth Sun came to be involves a god called Tecuciztecatl and another called Nanahuatzin, an eagle and a jaguar, a pyre and the sacrifice of hearts, but all of those belong to another story.

PACHACUTI: THE CYCLES OF TIME

• INCA •

THE SUN RISES AND SETS, the world spins, people live and die. Such are the cycles of time, which have endured through all the ages. Those who speak the Quechua tongue call this Pachacuti.

The age of the first Sun was born in the darkness of the beginning. The people then were primitive creatures, cousins to the *wari*, a beast which is part-llama, part-alpaca. Some of these people – the Wari Wiracocharuna – worshipped Viracocha, saying that he had made them; others said Pachacamac. Knowing no better, they clothed themselves in leaves.

The age of the second Sun belonged to the Wari Runa, the *wari* people, a race with a little more learning. Dressed in animal skins, they tended the soil and grew a few simple crops. Their god was Viracocha. A great flood ended their peaceful lives.

The age of the third Sun was a good time and a bad time. It belonged to the Purun Runa, the wild people. Their god was Pachacamac and they enjoyed the bounty he had provided. They spun wool into yarn and wove and coloured the yarn to make cloth for clothing. They planted and harvested their own crops. They mined the Earth for her hoard of gold, silver and precious stones, which they turned into jewellery and other fine ornaments. With good food in their bellies and warm clothes on their backs, they were healthy and strong and increased in number. Soon there was not enough space for them in their highland home and they spread out into the lowlands. But now, instead of sharing what they had, the people became afraid of losing it. Possessive, acquisitive and defensive –

of territory, of possessions – they banded together in towns, each under the rulership of a different king. For the first time, the people went to war with each other.

The age of the fourth Sun continued the mood of the third. This was the time of the Auca Runa, the warlike people. From their stone houses and fastnesses on the tops of mountains, they kept a lookout and guarded themselves against attack. Conflict and divisions marked this age. The people were divided into *ayllus*, kinship groups, according to their blood. The land, too, was divided; it became Tahuantinsuyu, the land of the four united quarters.

The age of the fifth Sun was the age of the glorious Inca empire, which stretched north, south, east and west across Tahuantinsuyu, over coastal desert, frozen mountain and fertile valley, and dazzled with its imperial wonders: its network of roads, which allowed for good communications and the rapid movement of troops; its irrigation systems, which brought water to a parched earth; its agricultural terraces, climbing up the hillsides like stairways for giants, which produced not only enough food for the multitude, but a surplus; its monumental buildings, erected without the benefit of iron tools or the wheel, and constructed of stones which interlock with such fine precision that barely a whisper can pass between them; its handicrafts in weaving and ceramics and jewellery and gold; and, presiding above it all, the High King himself, the Inca.

And yet how are even the most mighty fallen. In the Year of Our Lord 1532, on 24 September, rafts with huge, white wings came sailing down the coast. They landed, and those on board – a party of 168 and their leader, all pale-skinned, tall and bearded – disembarked, and made their way inland. 'Viracocha' was how the people described these alien beings. But they were not gods; they were men. Their leader was an unlettered pig farmer with a lust for gold. His name was Francisco Pizarro.

That day in 1532, when the Spanish galleons disembarked, marked the beginning of the end of the fifth Sun, the ending of the Inca world.

How the Gods Made the Sky-Earth

• MAYA •

Before the gods made *kajulew*, the sky-earth – plotting it like a field before cultivation and aligning its four corners with the midwinter and midsummer sunrise – before they did all of this, there was nothing. There were no people, no animals, no birds, no fish. No meadows, forests, valleys or mountains. There was only the sky above and *chopalo*, the lake-sea, pooled and calm, below.

The dark and empty universe pulsated with a silence as profound as infinity. In the lake-sea the quetzal feathers which clothed the gods of the water flashed blue-green, dusting the sea with a sprinkling of light. And in the sky, Hurricane, Heart of Heaven, gazed about at the void of the universe and fretted.

Descending to the lake-sea, Hurricane placed the problem which concerned him before Tepew Qukumatz, the Sovereign Plumed Serpent.

'How shall we sow the seeds of creation so that the dawn of creation may come?' he asked.

The two gods pondered, puzzled, debated and discussed, putting forward this argument and that, until finally it was agreed: the lake-sea would have to part to make way for the earth and then the rest of creation could follow.

Such was the power of the gods' words that they had only to say 'Earth' and it began to form, like swirling mist, before their eyes. Mountains rose out of the lake-sea, sculpting the earth's surface with their keen edges, sharp as a sacrificial knife. Forests grew on the land and the water that had collected in the gulleys and ravines became rivers and streams.

The gods looked at the work they had done and were pleased. The world lay before them – sky above, earth below, and around it the sea.

'It is good,' said Plumed Serpent to Hurricane, 'this world that we have created.'

The new world rumbled with sound, but it was not the kind of sound that the gods wished or needed to hear. Gods depend for their sustenance on words of worship and homage; praise to them is meat and drink. But in all the sounding universe not one word of praise could Hurricane and Plumed Serpent hear.

'How can we make beings who will feed us with prayers and nurture us with sacrifice?' they asked each other and, in the hope of receiving what they craved, they filled the uninhabited world with living creatures. They placed deer in the forests and pumas and jaguars, too. They placed snakes on the ground and birds in the treetops. Each creature had its own home and its own language.

'Speak!' said Plumed Serpent and Hurricane. 'Speak the names of those who have made you. Say you will glorify us and keep our holy days.'

But in reply all the animals did was to growl and hiss and howl and squawk and chatter and screech. The cacophony of sound was enough to give even a god a headache.

'This will not do,' said Hurricane and Plumed Serpent to the animals. 'Because you cannot speak the words we wish to hear, you must be of service to us in another way.' And that is why, ever since then, the animals have offered their flesh to be eaten as the gods commanded.

But still the gods were hungry for praise.

'How can we make beings who will feed us with prayers and nurture us with sacrifice?' they asked each other and they decided to try again.

Scooping up handfuls of mud, they moulded the raw material into the figure of a man. But the mud man was an awkward, ungainly thing with a crooked face and a stiff neck, which prevented his head from turning, and flesh as lumpen as the wet earth from which he was made.

'Speak!' said Plumed Serpent and Hurricane. 'Speak the names of those who have made you. Say you will glorify us and keep our holy days.'

But in reply all the mud man did was babble and burble and gibber. None of the words that he uttered made any sense at all. They flowed from his lopsided mouth in a stream as amorphous as his shapeless body, which was now beginning to disintegrate.

'This will not do!' said Hurricane and Plumed Serpent to each other. 'He cannot walk. He cannot reproduce, alone and by himself. From earth he came; to earth let him return. Let him be no more than a memory.'

As the gods looked on, the mud man slunk helplessly back into oblivion, seeping back into the clay from which he had come, legs, arms and torso surrendering to the earth and last of all his face, which gazed balefully at its creators as it dissolved into the formlessness of its beginnings.

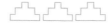

But still the gods were hungry for praise.

'How can we make beings who will feed us with prayers and nurture us with sacrifice?' they asked each other and decided to ask the help of Xpiyacoc and Xmucane. Grandfather Xpiyacoc was lord of the seeds of the coral tree; Grandmother Xmucane was keeper of the days, the mistress of time.

Grandmother and Grandfather began their divination. They took coral seeds and kernels of corn and cast them into lots, then counted off the days of the sacred calendar against each one. When the final lot was reached and the portent of its day revealed, Xpiyacoc and Xmucane, the divine Daykeepers, told the gods what they should do.

'Let it be done!' said Hurricane and Plumed Serpent, and at once it was. Before them stood two figures, one fashioned from the wood of the coral tree, the other from bulrushes. The first had every appearance of a man, the second every likeness to a woman. They had the power of speech too. They rapidly began to multiply, producing sons and daughters and peopling the sky-earth which the gods had made.

But although they looked like humans, the wooden mannikins were bloodless things, as dry as sticks, with unfeeling hearts and empty heads, unfilled with thoughts of gratitude, which rattled like withered gourds on top of their puppet bodies. In

THE CALENDAR

When the Spanish *conquistadors* arrived in the New World in the sixteenth century, they found that the calendar of the indigenous peoples of Mesoamerica was more precise than the Julian calendar then used in Europe. For the Maya, Aztecs and others, the calendar was much more than a record of the passing of time. It was also a map of the workings of Fate, and an essential tool in divination and prediction. It gave guidance on when to make sacrifice to the gods, when to plant or make war, and could be used, in hindsight, to justify the acts of kings.

The calendrical systems of the Mesoamericans were highly complex and involved not just one calendar but three, based largely on the cycles of the Sun, Moon and the planet Venus. The oldest and most important of these was the 260-day calendar, developed by the Zapotecs early in the first millennium BCE and known to the Maya and Aztecs respectively as the *tzolkin* – the 'sacred round' – and the *tonalpohualli*. A repeating cycle of 20 day names and 13 day numbers gave a total count of 260 days, equivalent to the length of a human pregnancy – it may well have been invented by midwives to calculate birth dates.

Each of the day names in this calendar belonged to a particular supernatural being and was often linked with a natural phenomenon as well. Both days and numbers were laden with prophetic meaning, making the 260-day calendar fundamental to the art of divination. Those who could interpret it – like Grandmother Xmucane of Maya myth (who, significantly, was also known as the divine midwife) – were, and are, referred to as 'daykeepers'. The 260-day calendar is still used by the highland Maya and in Oaxaca.

The second calendar was based on the solar year. It had 365 days and was divided into 18 months of 20 days. This left five days over which, existing in a kind of 'non-time', were called the *haab* and were considered unlucky.

The third and final calendar, used to record longer periods of time and perfected by the Maya, was the Long Count. It employed a basic unit of 360 days called a *tun*, and a numbering system based on 20. The largest cycle of time, a *baktun*, was equivalent to 400 *tuns*. By multiplying a *baktun* by 13, the Maya arrived at a Great Cycle, or 5130 years. The end of a Great Cycle signalled the cataclysmic destruction of the existing world and the birth of a new one.

The Great Cycle in which we live now began on the equivalent of 2 August 3114 BCE, and will finish on 23 December 2012. On that day, according to the Maya, the present world will end.

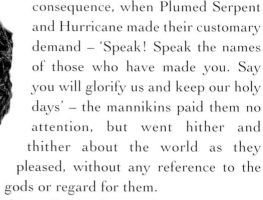

consequence, when Plumed Serpent and Hurricane made their customary demand – 'Speak! Speak the names of those who have made you. Say you will glorify us and keep our holy days' – the mannikins paid them no attention, but went hither and thither about the world as they pleased, without any reference to the gods or regard for them.

'This will not do!' said Hurricane and Plumed Serpent to each other. They decided to destroy what they had made and the destruction was terrible indeed. A great rain began to fall. It was a deluge not of water but of burning resin – the sap of trees. So dense was it that it turned the sky black, and in the darkness all of creation turned upon the wooden mannikins. Wild beasts entered their houses, a sure sign of the gods' anger. Ferocious creatures attacked them, gouging out their eyes, biting off their heads, tearing apart their bodies, crunching their bones. Even their everyday utensils, those objects made for domestic use – plates and pots and jars and griddles and grinding stones – suddenly sprang to life and set upon them in revenge for the abuse they had endured.

'You burned us on the fire and gave us nothing but pain,' cried the pots and the griddles. 'Now it is your turn to feel pain!'

'You ground us down, wore us down, scraped and crushed us against each other,' cried the grinding stones. 'Now it is your turn to be crushed!'

'You starved and beat us and ate us,' cried the dogs and the turkeys, joining in the chorus of accusation. 'Now it is your turn to be eaten!'

And as dogs and turkeys and pots and griddles and grinding stones pounded and bit and broke and smashed the wooden puppets, the hearths of all the fireplaces exploded and the hearthstones flew at the heads of the mannikins. Three stones from one hearth, blasted beyond the confines of the earth, came to rest in the sky, where they were transformed into three stars in the constellation Orion.

As the cataclysm raged, nowhere could the mannikins find any shelter.

They clambered on to the tops of the houses, but the houses collapsed.

They climbed into the trees, but the trees shook them off.

They ran for the caves, but the caves shut in their faces.

That is how the world of the wooden race ended. The only remaining sign that they ever existed are the monkeys who chatter mindlessly in the forests, for they are their descendants.

The storm was stilled, the sky-earth was at peace and the time was drawing near when the Sun and Moon would rise for the first time. Yet still the world was without people. Still the gods were hungry for praise. So they sent Fox, Coyote, Parrot and Crow out into the world to find the one substance from which human bones and flesh could be made.

The animals found it at the mountain called *pan paxil*, Split Place, *pan kayala*, Bitter Water Place. Inside the belly of the mountain was a hoard of all the fruits of the earth, an aromatic larder of all that is good to eat. There were pods of cacao from which chocolate is made, velvet-skinned sapotas, luscious custard apples and numerous other succulent fruits, seeds and kernels. There was corn, too, both yellow and white, and it was this that the animals brought back to the gods.

Grandmother Xmucane took the ears of yellow corn and white corn and ground them nine times on her grinding stone, breaking open the kernels and pounding them until they were as fine as the finest powder. As she worked, she rinsed her hands with water to remove the sticky meal.

Then Plumed Serpent took the cornmeal which

43

Xmucane had made and began to mould it into shape. The water from the grinding became blood. The meal mixed with water became fat. And as Plumed Serpent modelled and pinched the cornmeal paste, he created the first human beings.

The corn people were perfect in every way. Their skin was golden, their hair glossy and black, their eyes clear, their gait sure, their words lucid.

'Speak!' said Plumed Serpent and Hurricane. 'Speak the names of those who have made you. Say that you will glorify us and that you will keep our holy days.'

In reply, the corn people bowed down before the gods and offered up them prayers and tributes and thanked them for their birth, and the creators were at last rewarded and felt happy.

But the corn people were perhaps a little too perfect, their eyes a little too clear. They could see everything there was to see, on earth, under the ocean and in the rolling heavens. Their vision extended to the far reaches of the universe and nothing – mountains, forests, lakes, land – could impede it. They looked through everything as if it were glass and the more they looked the more they knew.

'This will never do,' said Hurricane and Plumed Serpent to each other. 'Their eyes are open and soon they will be as gods.' So the creators sent a mist to cloud the corn people's vision and prevent them from seeing too far, like breath that clouds a mirror. So it was for the corn people and so it is for us. Never will we have full understanding. Never will we know all there is to know or see all there is to see, for the gods have misted our eyes.

> *Truly now,*
> *double thanks, triple thanks*
> *that we've been formed, we've been given*
> *our mouths, our faces,*
> *we speak, we listen,*
> *we wonder, we move,*
> *our knowledge is good, we've understood*
> *what is far and near,*
> *and we've seen what is great and small*
> *under the sky, on the earth.*
> *Thanks to you we've been formed,*
> *we've come to be made and modeled,*
> *our grandmother, our grandfather*

From *Popul Vuh*

Sacred Hallucinogens

Certain plants, now debased to the status of mere drugs in the West, were once sacred substances for the peoples of old Mexico and the Inca empire, opening the doors of perception and allowing communion with the gods. Psilocybin mushrooms, *Psilocybe mexicana*, were one such plant.

According to Mixtec legend, the sacred fungus was given to the gods by Nine Wind, the Mixtec counterpart of Ehecatl-Quetzalcoatl, and is personified by two goddesses, Four Lizard and Eleven Lizard. The Aztecs are known to have eaten psilocybin mushrooms mixed with honey, after which they would have visions in which they would see portents of the future. The use of the psilocybin mushroom may be very ancient, going back more than 2000 years into the Late Preclassic period (300 BCE–100 CE) of the Maya. Small, mushroom-shaped stone sculptures have been found at such Preclassic sites as Kaminaljuyú, along with grinding stones which recall those used by modern-day Mixtecs in Oaxaca to break down the mushroom before taking it.

The seeds of the morning glory, *Turbina corymbosa* – known as *ololiuhqui* in the Aztec language Nahuatl – were another important ecstatic substance. In their nocturnal divinations, seers would make contact with the highly revered *ololiuhqui* god, who would reveal to them the information they sought.

Tobacco (*Nicotiana* spp.) was widely used in Mesoamerica, in one of two ways. Ground and mixed with powdered lime, the leaf was chewed to heighten the intoxicating effects of the nicotine, and to reduce fatigue during lengthy vigils. It was also smoked in cigars – a word which derives from the Maya *sikar*, meaning cigar or tobacco – or in pipes. Like the rearing Vision Serpent of the bloodletting ritual (see page 87), the rising column of smoke provided a conduit between the worlds of humans and gods. To the Aztecs, tobacco was believed to be either the embodiment or creation of the goddess of the Milky Way.

In Peru, heartland of the old Inca empire, the leaves of coca, the plant from which cocaine is derived, were – and are – chewed, or given as marriage or funerary gifts. Among the Incas, its use was confined to those of royal blood, the priestly caste, and healers. Chewing the leaves enabled Inca messengers to travel up to 250 kilometres (155 miles) a day. Initially condemned by the Spanish Church as a 'delusion of the devil', it was soon realized that the practice had its benefits to the colonists. Chewing coca dulled the senses against cold and exhaustion and allowed the indigenous labour force in the mines and on the plantations to survive the harsh working conditions. As a result, the Church soon established a monopoly in the production of the crop, conjuring the ironic image of the Catholic Church as sixteenth-century drug barons.

THE DEER GODS, THE WIND GODS AND THE WORLD

• MIXTEC •

IN THE DARK TIME, Grandfather and Grandmother One Deer, by the power of their magic, raised a mountain out of the sea. It was called Place Where the Heavens Stand. On its peak they placed a copper axe, blade upward, to prop up the sky.

Grandmother One Deer and Grandfather One Deer built themselves a fine palace on the mountain, near the site of sacred Apoala. Here they lived, more than halfway to heaven on the mountainside, for many a long year.

But one day their solitude was ended, for two sons were born to them. Named after the days of their birth, they were called Wind of Nine Snakes and Wind of Nine Caves and they could alter their shape at will. One could be an eagle who soars like the Sun. The other could be a feathery, flying snake, a bird-serpent for whom stone was as permeable as the sky.

Wind of Nine Snakes and Wind of Nine Caves set to and made a magic garden on a little piece of land. In it they planted fruit trees and sweet herbs and all the flowers and plants beloved of the gods – golden marigold and yarrow, blue morning glory with its seeds of revelation, the dreaming mushroom, tobacco with its sacred smoke.

The brothers tilled and tended their garden and then, on a small grassy plot to the side, they prepared to make an offering. They picked tobacco leaves and dried them, then packed them into clay vessels and set them alight. Sweet-scented spirals of hazy blue coiled their way towards heaven and reached the nostrils of Grandfather and Grandmother One Deer.

'Mm-mm,' they murmured and 'Aah!' they sighed and, inhaling deeply, drifted off into dreams in the cloud of tobacco smoke, sweet-smelling and mellow.

This was the first offering ever made to the gods.

Down below, Wind of Nine Snakes and Wind of Nine Caves were praying: 'Let the light come. Let all the land be uncovered. Let the water be gathered. Let the Earth be peopled.'

And to give power to their prayers, they pierced their ears and their tongues with blades of flint and dripped their blood on the trees and flowers, using brushes made of willow.

As the brothers wished, so it was. The dawn came. The sea withdrew from the land. The water collected in gulleys and pooled into lakes. A new people appeared to live on Earth.

But this was not the only race to inhabit the Earth. The first people came from the deepest places in rock and cave. When the first Sun arose, it froze them to stone. Later another race, who were gods and rulers, came from the hearts of trees. The trees grew near sacred Apoala, where the palace of One Deer stood.

COSMIC POWERS

THE UNIVERSE IS FILLED with natural phenomena which, in their raw might and awe-inspiring power, make the human race seem insignificant. Nowadays, with our foolish arrogance and faith in the powers of science, we believe we can manipulate nature without consequence. Ancient peoples, however, took a more holistic view: they saw themselves as part of nature and had a healthy reverence for the powers on which their survival depended. Natural phenomena – the Sun, Moon and Stars, Wind, Rain and Thunder, the Rainbow, even the Earth itself – were all personified as gods or goddesses and worshipped under various names.

For the peoples of Mesoamerica and the old Inca empire, the Sun, the Moon, the planet Venus and the Pleiades were particularly important. The Sun of the fifth Aztec age – our present one – was the dreaded Tonatiuh, who demanded blood sacrifice before he would move across the skies. For the Incas the Sun god Inti, or Apu Punchau, was originally the supreme deity, but later his position was usurped by the creator god Viracocha. The Sun's sister-wife Mama Quilla was the Moon. On the earthly plane, the Inca emperor and his wife were considered the flesh-and-blood embodiments of the Sun and Moon. The cycle of the Pleiades was associated with agricultural seasons.

Venus was especially closely observed. Known to the Incas as Chasca, the Sun's attendant, the planet had various names among the Mesoamericans. The most famous of these was Quetzalcoatl, who was god of Venus as the Morning Star (his twin the Evening Star is sometimes known as Xolotl). As Maya astronomers realized early on, the Morning and Evening Stars are the same body – Venus – in two separate phases. As 'morning star', Venus appears before the Sun, and was thought to lead the Sun out of the underworld; as 'evening star', seen just after sunset, it was thought to be harrying the Sun back into the underworld. The planet's dual aspect meant that its influence could be either benign or malign, as is seen in the myth of Hunahpu and Xbalanque.

THE FIFTH SUN

• AZTEC •

FOUR AGES HAD COME and gone, four Suns risen and set. Now was the beginning of the fifth age. The gods, anxious for a new dawn, gathered together at Teotihuacan.

'Who will be the fifth Sun?' they asked. 'Who among us will take on the job of lighting the world?'

'I will!' cried Tecuciztecatl, his mind dazzled with images of glory.

But some of the gods were unsure. 'Is there anyone else?' they called. No other volunteers came forward.

At the back of the crowd stood Nanahuatzin, sickly, ugly, puny and pitiful.

'You!' they cried. 'What about you?'

Nanahuatzin looked around. There was no mistaking it: the gods were addressing him. 'Well … since you ask … if that is your wish,' he replied and, like a warrior who goes to the forefront of battle, he accepted the obligation and honour conferred on him.

The gods raised two hills where Tecuciztecatl and Nanahuatzin could fast and purify themselves in preparation for their fate. The hills still stand at Teotihuacan. They are called the Pyramids of the Sun and Moon.

At the same time, the gods built a great bonfire and set it alight. On this the two rivals would give their lives, for death is the prerequisite of rebirth and the new Sun could only be born in the travails of sacrifice.

For four days the pyre burned, hotter and hotter. For four days the pair continued their ritual of purification, letting blood and making offerings. Those of Tecuciztecatl were sumptuous beyond belief. In place of the customary fir boughs he brought quetzal feathers of iridescent hues. In place of the sacred bundles of bound grass in which lay the tools of bloodletting, he gave balls of gold. In place of flesh-piercing maguey thorns tipped with his own blood, he gave spines of jade tipped with coral. And as for his incense, it was the finest, the costliest, the most fragrant.

What could the lowly Nanahuatzin offer to match this show of splendour? Nothing but what he had. His fir branches and grass balls were bundles of reeds. His maguey thorns were just that, dipped in the blood of his own body. And as for incense he had none, so instead he used the scabs from his own scar-encrusted skin.

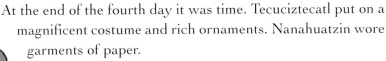

At the end of the fourth day it was time. Tecuciztecatl put on a magnificent costume and rich ornaments. Nanahuatzin wore garments of paper.

The gods encircled the blazing pyre: 'Jump!' they shouted. 'Jump!'

Tecuciztecatl ran towards the fire. The flames were flickering tongues waiting to suck him in, the searing heat a barrier he could not cross. Fear filled his being. Again he tried. And again and again, four times without success.

Now the lowly Nanahuatzin, least glorious of all the gods, stepped forward. Shutting his eyes so they would not see and closing his mind to all thoughts of pain, he broke into a run. He did not stop. He did not falter. He did not trip. He hurled himself on to the pyre and was immolated in the flames.

Shamed, Tecuciztecatl at last followed, then the eagle and jaguar too. Charred by the fire, the tips of the eagle's wings blackened and the jaguar's golden pelt was spotted with soot. In memory of this brave act, the eagle and jaguar became the emblems of the two great orders of Aztec warriors. But all that came later, after the dawning.

As the last flames guttered and died and darkness prevailed, the gods waited, looking this way and that for signs of change. Slowly, in the east, the sky began to redden. Like a ball of fire, Nanahuatzin erupted from the horizon, shooting out burning rays in every direction and lighting the whole world – Nanahuatzin, metamorphosed by death. He had a new name now. He was Tonatiuh, the Sun. His face was red, his hair golden, and a halo encircled his head. So incandescent was he that the gods could not look in his face.

A moment later he was followed by Tecuciztecatl, round, brilliant and bright, a second Sun to rival Tonatiuh in splendour.

This was not what the gods wanted. 'Stop!' they shouted. 'Dim your light!' But, proud and unheeding, Tecuciztecatl glared on.

As the gods were deliberating, a rabbit came hopping by. Without further thought, one of them seized it and hurled it at his shining face. Splattered there, the rabbit obscured his light and Tecuciztecatl, the second Sun, became the Moon. Still, on nights when the Moon is full, the rabbit's imprint can be seen.

High in the heavens, Sun and Moon hovered, motionless.

'Move!' screamed the gods. But Tonatiuh refused. 'Blood!' he roared. 'Give me your blood and your hearts!'

Outraged that Tonatiuh should demand such a sacrifice of his peers, the Morning Star fired a dart at him. The dart missed its mark and the Sun, in retaliation, fired one of his own. It pierced Morning Star through the head and he became Itztlacoliuhqui, a god as cold as stone. From that moment on, when the Morning Star rises at dawn he spreads his coldness about him.

To make the Sun move, the gods realized they would have to surrender to his demand. And so, one by one, they came to die, baring their breasts to Quetzalcoatl, who gouged out their hearts with a sacrificial knife. Their ornaments, their cloaks, their finery, no longed needed, were wrapped up to make *tlaquimilolli,* sacred bundles, the divine relics through which humans can worship the gods.

When all had been slain, Tonatiuh, satiated by his bloody feast, at last began to move.

Such was the sacrifice that took place at Teotihuacan.

The Sun of Motion is Nahui Ollin, the Sun of the fifth age, in which we still live. To ensure that he continues to move, we, like the gods, must feed him our hearts and our blood.

THE PLUMED SERPENT AND THE MORNING STAR

• AZTEC •

WHEN QUETZALCOATL THE Plumed Serpent appeared on Earth, he brought with him knowledge of many things. He showed the people the patterns of time, governed by the Sun, and gave them a sacred calendar whose days and years contained the signs of divination. He gave them maize so that they would not go hungry. He taught them different skills so that they became adept in writing, in gold- and silver-smithing, in jewel-work, in healing.

His people were the Toltecs and the city he founded was called Tula, or Tollan, City of the Sun. Here Quetzalcoatl, the Toltecs' high priest and first king, lived in a palace

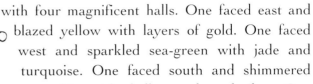

with four magnificent halls. One faced east and blazed yellow with layers of gold. One faced west and sparkled sea-green with jade and turquoise. One faced south and shimmered white with shells, pearls and silver. One faced north and burned red with shells and bloodstones. A mighty river flowed below this wonderful palace, through the heart of the city, and every night at midnight the great priest-king would go down to the river to bathe; and the place where he did this was called In the Precious Waters.

It was truly a golden age and under the beneficent rule of good King Quetzalcoatl the Toltecs of Tula prospered and were happy.

But it was not to last.

Quetzalcoatl had an enemy, bent on his destruction; where he sowed peace, his foe fomented discord; where he was benign, his foe was full of trickery; where he was a quetzal bird, his foe was a cat, the jaguar of the night.

And so it was, one day, that this lord of misrule, this god of an alien race, came to Tula. By his side were two others. In his hand was a mirror of black volcanic glass – obsidian – a scryer's toy. His name was Tezcatlipoca and in his Smoking Mirror could be seen the shadows of what was to come.

'Go!' said Tezcatlipoca to Quetzalcoatl's servants. 'Tell your master that I have come to show him his flesh.'

'What do you mean, "show me my flesh"?' asked the bird-king when the sorcerer was brought into his presence.

'My lord,' replied the wily Tezcatlipoca, 'I come to offer you what very few are granted – to see yourself as you truly are.' And he held up his mirror.

What Quetzalcoatl saw, reflected in the polished black obsidian, was the irrevocable decay of human flesh, as inevitable as the grave; his face was that of an old, old man. His skin was pale and puckered with lines and wrinkles. His lids were red, his rheumy eyes sunken. From his chin hung a long, white beard.

He leapt back, horrified.

'How hideous I am! How can my people look upon me without fear? I must leave – I must not inflict such ugliness on them a moment longer!'

'My lord, but you are too hard on yourself! You have had a shock. Here, sip this – it may ease your suffering.' And Tezcatlipoca offered him an intoxicating drink made from the fermented sap of the maguey plant. It was *pulque*, which, on this occasion, had been laced with magic mushroom.

Quetzalcoatl refused. 'I am sick.'

But Tezcatlipoca persisted. 'Just a little taste? Try some on the tip of your finger. What harm can that do?'

The bird-king took a small amount on the tip of his finger, licked it – and was lost. Seizing the goblet from his guest's hand, he swallowed its contents in one single gulp. Then he sent for his sister, Quetzalpetlatl, who lived on Mount Nonoalco. She too tried the sorceror's brew and became as inebriated as her brother.

That night, lost to all reason, the pair did not perform their devotions nor did they bathe, but instead they lay together until dawn.

When Quetzalcoatl awoke in the cold light of day and saw what he had done, he was greatly ashamed.

'I am not fit to rule my people. Let them make me a chamber underground where I will rest. Then I will go to Tlapallan, to the Land of Red Daylight, from which I came.'

So it was done. After four days in the darkness, Quetzalcoatl rose. When he looked on Tula, he wept.

'Watch for me in the east,' he told the Toltec people. 'One day, some day, I will return.'

Then he burned his fabulous palace, buried his treasures of gold and silver in the mountains and the ravines, turned his cacao trees, his chocolate trees, into mesquite bushes, and sent his birds, his jewel-coloured quetzal birds, ahead to guide his way. When he had finished, he placed his foot on the road and left.

As he journeyed eastwards, he stopped to rest at a place called Quauhtitlan, at the foot of a great tree. Its shape was gnarled, its bark cracked and lined, just like his face. 'I am an old man,' he said. From that time, the place was named Huehuequauhtitlan. It was the place of the Tree of Old Age.

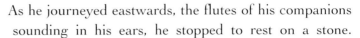

As he journeyed eastwards, the flutes of his companions sounding in his ears, he stopped to rest on a stone. Looking back, he saw Tula, shining Tula, and he began to weep. His tears coursed in rivers down his old cheeks and melted the stone on which he sat, etching in its hard face the furrows of grief. The imprint of his hands and body stayed in the stone, too, so that from that time the place was known as Temacpalco, the Mark of the Hands.

As he travelled eastwards, he came to a place called Coaapan, where he was met by evil gods who were enemies of the Toltecs.

'Where are you going', they asked, 'and why?'

'Give us your secrets,' they said, 'of gold- and silver-smithing, of feather-weaving, of jewel-work, of carving, of painting, of illumination – reveal to us the crafts of man's hand and the treasures of his imagination.' And Quetzalcoatl shed these secrets, for he had no use for them now: the past fell from him like the sloughed skin of a snake. Then he took the jewelled collar from around his neck and threw it into the water, so that from that time the place was known as Cozcaapa, the Water of Precious Stones.

As he travelled eastwards, he met a sorceror, a shaman. 'Where are you going,' he asked, 'and why?' And he forced Quetzalcoatl to take a drink of *pulque* so that he dropped down where he stood and fell into an unrousable, rumbling sleep. When he awoke, there was nothing but silence and emptiness around him, and from that time the place was known as the City of Sleepers. It was Cochtan.

As he travelled eastwards, he passed between a volcano and the Mountain of Snow. Here the snow fell, snow on snow, on Quetzalcoatl and his dwarves, his humpbacks and clowns – his blameless, faithful companions – so that all, save he, were frozen to death. The weight of this sorrow almost broke his heart, and he sang a lament that floated over the mountains like the cry of a desolate bird.

As he travelled eastwards, he came at last to Mount Poyauhtecatl, the Hill of Many Colours. On the other side of the mountain was the sea.

By the shore he made himself a raft of serpents and sailed away on it to Tlapallan, to the Land of Red Daylight.

ARTS AND CRAFTS

The Toltecs, whose god and first king was Quetzalcoatl, were regarded as supreme artisans by their successors the Aztecs. One craft which the Toltecs, who rose to power in the Early Postclassic period (900–1200 CE), established in Mesoamerica was that of gold-working, a skill which was not developed in the region until comparatively late.

For the Aztecs, gold was *teocuitlatl*, or excrement of the gods. Aztec goldsmiths were highly esteemed, and known as *teocuitlahuaque*; their patron god was Xipe Totec. Few of their artefacts survived the Spanish Conquest. Two that did, however, give some idea of the scale of their abilities. These consisted of a pair of discs, a staggering 1.8 metres (6 feet) wide, one in gold representing the Sun and the other in silver representing the Moon.

Gold had been worked in South America for millennia before the secrets of the craft spread northwards. The real triumph of Inca art was to be found at the Coricancha, the Temple of the Sun, at Cuzco. The walls here were laminated with 700 sheets of gold studded with emeralds and turquoise, and the windows were so placed that the Sun's rays would ignite the walls with a blinding light. There was golden statuary, too: according to legend, part of the ransom offered to the Spanish by the Inca Atahualpa in exchange for his life was twenty life-sized golden statues.

In Mesoamerica jade was valued more than gold. Perhaps because of its colouring, it was associated with water, the sky, vegetation and the precious feathers of the quetzal bird. It was extremely hard and was often worked with jade tools, and abraded with powdered jade or quartz sand. The Olmecs (*c.* 1200 BCE), were the first to carve it and used it to make masks, images of gods, and ritual utensils. Turquoise was another treasured stone, but is not seen until the Toltecs.

The jewel-like feathers of tropical birds were also highly prized. In the Inca empire, specially chosen women spent their time weaving capes, or *mantas*, from these feathers for the Inca and his priests – in Cuzco, there was a feather storehouse to supply them. Aztec craftworkers also used feathers to make cloaks, headdresses and other garments.

In Mesoamerica cloth was woven from the fibres of the cotton plant. Since this was women's work, it came under the patronage of particular goddesses. In Maya *codices* from Yucatan, both the young Goddess I and the old Goddess O are shown as weavers. The Aztec goddess Tlazolteotl wore a headdress of unspun cotton adorned with two spindles.

The Incas in the hot coastal lowlands favoured garments of cool cotton, but in the colder highlands cloth was woven from llama or alpaca wool. The wool of the vicuña, the softest of all, was reserved for the emperor, who wore his robes only once, after which they were ceremonially burnt. Meaningful designs were woven into the royal cloth, but we no longer know how to interpret them.

Or, by the shore, he built a bonfire and threw himself upon it. His body burned to ashes, but his heart, accompanied by wheeling, rainbow-coloured birds, rose into the sky, where it became Venus, the Morning Star, who leads the Sun from hiding. Learned astronomers have calculated the date of this occurrence, when flesh was transfigured to light, when the divine king died. It took place, they say, on the sixteenth day of July in the Year of Our Lord 750, when the Sun's face was eclipsed and Venus was seen close by.

Quetzalcoatl has not died, the once-and-future king. He is but dreaming, in the sunset land in the west. One day he will rise again. One day.

Seven Macaw and the Four Hundred Boys

• MAYA •

THE EVENTS IN THE HISTORY that follows happened long, long ago – so long ago, in fact, that even the Sun had not yet been born. The world was not totally dark, however, but glowed with a dim light cast by the lustrous feathers and glittering emerald teeth of Vucub Caquix, Seven Macaw. The people of this age – a dull and stupid race of wooden mannikins who later came to a sorry but well-deserved end – worshipped Seven Macaw, believing in their ignorance that he was the true Light of Heaven.

Seven Macaw, whose feathers were said to be seven times brighter than fire, revelled in their adulation and, indeed, encouraged it with false boasts and shameless lies.

'I am the greatest! I am the Sun and the Moon!' he proclaimed.

Seven Macaw had a wife, whose name was Chimalmat, and two sons.

The first of these was Zipacna, Earth-heaper. He was a maker of mountains and had, in a single night, piled up enough soil and rocks and boulders to raise no fewer than six mighty peaks.

'I am the greatest! I am the Maker of the Earth!' he proclaimed.

The second son was Cabrakan, Earth-shaker. What his brother piled up, he had the power to bring down. When he shuddered he made the Earth shake, opening fissures in her face and causing hills and mountains to tumble. 'I am the greatest! I can bring down the sky!' he proclaimed.

Clearly the boastful ways of the father flourished in his sons.

The lies of Seven Macaw and his offspring reached the ears of Hurricane, Heart of Heaven, and he decided to send two emissaries to silence them once and for all. They were Hunahpu and Xbalanque, the divine hero-twins.

Now Seven Macaw had a prized nance tree, a tapal tree of a type that grows on the edge of the rainforest and on the savanna, which bears small, round, aromatic yellow fruit, and he was in the habit of visiting it every day to feed. It was therefore easy for Hunahpu and Xbalanque to find him.

Hiding themselves in the tree, they waited, and soon saw their quarry approaching. When Seven Macaw was comfortably settled in the uppermost branches, Hunahpu raised his blowgun and fired. His poisoned dart flew unerringly towards its target and pierced Seven Macaw in the mouth, cracking his jaw and spreading venom through his veins. He fell out of the tree and crashed on to the ground below.

At once Hunahpu was upon him. But the monster grabbed his arm and bent it back, all the way to the shoulder, and tore it right out of its socket.

Cradling his jaw with one hand and holding the bleeding arm in another, Seven Macaw hurried home.

'What has happened to you?' said Chimalmat when she saw him.

Her husband could hardly speak for the pain.

'Ouch! Aah! My jaw! My teeth! I'm in agony. Don't make me talk!' And he gave her Hunahpu's arm, which she placed on a spit over the fire, where it slowly turned and roasted.

The hero-twins, meanwhile, were hatching a plot to retrieve the missing arm. They consulted a pair of healers, an elderly, bow-backed, white-haired couple by the names of Great White Hog and Great White Raccoon. The couple agreed to help them and they all set out for Seven Macaw's house.

Great White Hog and Great White Raccoon tottered along the road towards it, with Hunahpu and Xbalanque, in disguise, skipping along behind them like carefree little children. As they drew closer, they saw Seven Macaw sitting in front of it, nursing his toothache.

'Where are you going, Grandfather?' he said, just managing to speak.

'We are travelling healers, your lordship. That is how we earn our living.'

'But Grandfather, you are old. Why do you work when you have children to support you?' replied Seven Macaw, indicating the boys behind them.

'Oh, please excuse them, your lordship – be quiet, you two! No, they are not our children. They are our grandchildren and they follow us everywhere. What can we do? They have no one in the world but us. And so we go on, working to keep us all, curing teeth and healing eyes and setting bones.'

'You cure teeth? What medicines can you give me for mine? I cannot eat, I cannot sleep – my suffering is intolerable. Please help me,' said Seven Macaw.

The trap had been sprung and the prey had fallen right into it.

'Well, your lordship,' replied Great White Hog, 'the cause of your toothache is a worm that gnaws at the bone. To pull out the worm, we must pull out your teeth.'

'My teeth!' cried Seven Macaw, the shock of this suggestion overcoming the excruciating pain of moving his jaw in speech. 'But I am a great lord – I am the Sun that lights the day! I cannot go about toothless. My teeth and my eyes are my best features!'

'Never fear, your lordship – we will replace your teeth with false ones made from ground bone. No one will know the difference.'

And so the dentistry began. One by one, Great White Hog and Great White Raccoon extracted all of Seven Macaw's glittering emerald teeth. In the cavities left by the precious stones they inserted beads of a creamy-white substance. These were not ground bone, of course; the new false teeth were kernels of corn, as useless for biting and chewing as rubbery lumps of dough. His cheeks hollow, his lips sunken, Seven Macaw looked like a toothless old man whose face has imploded into the recesses of his skull.

Then the healers went to work on his eyes, pulling away the glowing discs that surrounded them. When they were done, only bare patches of white remained (which is why, to this day, the scarlet macaw has white patches around its eyes).

Seven Macaw was a shadow of his former self. His glory extinguished like a burnt-out flame, he gave up the spirit and died. He ascended to the northern sky, where he was transformed into the seven stars which make up the Big Dipper. His wife Chimalmat joined him there, changed in death into a circle of stars which form part of the Little Dipper.

Rescued from the fire, Hunahpu's arm was reinserted in its socket, and such were the bone-knitting skills of the two ancient healers that the limb rooted itself perfectly back into place, with not so much as a scar remaining in memory of the wound.

Now that Seven Macaw was dead, only Zipacna and Cabrakan remained.

Zipacna the Earth-piler was floating gently by the shore. His long reptilian form was just submerged in the water and only his watchful eyes and nose protruded, like the tips of rocks jutting above the surface. As he lay there, inert but alert, who should come along but the Four Hundred Boys, dragging what looked like an entire tree trunk behind them.

Zipacna's interest was aroused. He decided to investigate further. Sliding noiselessly out of the water, he crawled after them.

'What are you doing with that tree?' he asked when he caught up with them.

'It is a post for the house we are building, but it is so heavy we cannot lift it.'

'Oh, it is nothing for one such as I,' said boastful Zipacna, and he raised the log and set it in place as if it were no heavier than a feather.

'Did you see that?' the Boys whispered to each other. 'There are four hundred of us and only one of him – yet he did what we could not. Such strength is dangerous. We must get rid of him.' And they thought of a plan.

They began digging a deep trench, for the foundations of their house, they said. After a hour or two's work, they downed tools. 'Ooh,' they said, rubbing their backs

and massaging their shoulders and making a great show of their exhaustion, 'how tired we are! We cannot go on a moment longer. You are so strong. Will you take over?'

Zipacna was indeed strong – strong, but not stupid. So, when the Boys asked him to dig the trench, he knew that in fact what they were asking him to do was to dig his own grave. He agreed to take part in the charade – revenge could come later – and, as a safety measure, he dug a small tunnel in the wall of the trench in which he could hide.

'How are you doing down there? Let us know when you're finished. And make sure you do a tidy job – we can't be clearing up after you, you know.' It was easy to scold when the Earth-piler was such a safe distance away.

When Zipacna called out that he had done, the Boys put the second part of their plan into action. They hauled a huge log to the edge and with a mighty heave – *one – two – three* – hurled it down into the pit. But no sound came back to them. No crunching of skull bones, no scream of pain. What was going on down there?

At last, as if from another dimension, they heard the echo of a distant cry, far away, so far away. The log had hit its target: the monster in the pit was dead! Now this was cause for serious celebration. And if there was one thing that the Four Hundred Boys knew how to do, it was celebrate, for they were the gods of intoxicating liquor, and had in their keeping the recipe for a particularly delicious and potent drink made from the sap of the maguey plant. And this they now set about brewing.

'The ants will strip his bones bare,' they said to each other, 'and when we see them, we will toast our victory with our drink – our sweet drink.'

The first day went by, the second day. Now it was the third and the Four Hundred Boys watched as columns of ants emerged from the trench, bearing in their strong little mandibles scraps of hair and snippets of toenail, collected, they were sure, from the decaying body of Zipacna deep down in the pit.

Oh, how they rejoiced. How they danced. How they drank. And in no time at all, their sweet drink had worked its intoxicating magic and they were all incoherently, hopelessly and helplessly drunk.

Their revelry was, however, premature. Deep down in the pit Zipacna was not dead, but waiting. All this time, in his tunnel, he had been pulling out strands of hair and biting off pieces of nail to give to the ants to carry out as proof of his death. Now that the Four Hundred Boys were beyond sense and reason came the moment for revenge. Summoning all his mountain-making strength, the Earth-piler heaved and the entire structure above him – logs, roof-timbers, lintels, posts, crossbeams – came crashing down on the Four Hundred Boys and catapulted them into space, where they were transformed into the stars known as the Pleiades. Tossed like a handful of seeds into the sky, they have remained there ever since, marking the turning of the seasons: when the Pleiades sink behind the western horizon, the people know that it is time to sink their seeds into the soil.

Hunahpu and Xbalanque grieved for the loss of the Four Hundred Boys. Their mission, to relieve the world of Seven Macaw and his descendants, still stood.

Zipacna, they knew, spent his days looking for fish and crabs, which were the foods on which he fed. But of late his fishing expeditions had yielded nothing and it was now two full days since the great cayman lord had had a square meal. Visions tormented him: plump fish; whiskered fish; elongated fish which moved like snakes through the water; little fish that swam in shoals; fish with firm, white flesh, with meaty, red flesh. He dreamed, too, of shellfish that clung to rocks, or moved sideways in the shallows on their articulated legs and peered out at the world from little black eyes.

Zipacna was ravenous; the promise of food, Hunahpu and Xbalanque decided, was the bait that would hook this particular catch.

So they set about making a model of a giant crab. Bromeliad flowers from the rainforest masqueraded as front legs; the red bracts, which fanned out like a pineapple crest around the flower panicles, were the pretended claws. A large flagstone served as a shell.

Leaving the false crab tucked away out of sight in a crevice beneath the overhang of a great cliff, her flower legs protruding, they went looking for Zipacna. They found him by the bank, staring morosely into the clear and fish-free water.

'Good-day, friend. Are you looking for a catch? We can tell you where to find an excellent one – a giant crab. We would have caught her ourselves, but she was so enormous that she scared us away.'

'Don't tell me where she is. Show me! Are you men or not?' replied Zipacna, with a lewd chuckle.

Hunahpu and Xbalanque led him westwards to the cliff where, hidden deep in the crevice, the crab lay, red and glistening.

'There!' they said. 'There she is – can't you see her, with her legs sticking out? You'll have to go in to get her.'

As soon Zipacna saw the crab, he just had to have her! Nothing else would satisfy his lust. Lowering himself, he wriggled into position and began to work his way in. Ooh, aah, that hurt … perhaps this way … no, that way. It was extremely difficult – but then he had never done it before. Suddenly the crab seemed to be on top of him and upside-down – surely that couldn't be right? He would have to try another position. On his back perhaps?

This time he was successful. He penetrated deep, deep into the mountain, until only his kneecaps were showing. 'Aaah …' He gave a sigh of profound satisfaction. And, as he did so, the rock mass above him closed in on him, and he was metamorphosed into eternal stone.

Zipacna was dead.

That left only Cabrakan.

With the lightest tap of his foot this Cabrakan, the Earth-shaker, could bring whole mountains tumbling down. It would never do: he must be stopped. Hunahpu and Xbalanque set off to find him.

'Good-day, friend,' they said when they saw him. 'And how are you?'

'I am the greatest! Can you not see? I am the breaker of mountains, I am the scatterer of rocks, I am …'

The twins cut him short. 'If you are such a mighty breaker of mountains, then how is it that there's a mountain in the east which you haven't touched? It's getting bigger day by day, minute by minute; it's rising above all the rest.'

A mountain he had missed? Cabrakan was stunned and angry.

'Take me there at once,' he said, and so the three set off, with the Earth-piler in the middle.

As they made their way eastward, Hunahpu and Xbalanque brought down several birds with their blowgun. They stopped and made a fire, plucked the birds and set them to roast. The flames crackled with the dripping fat, and the heat sent the meat's succulent aroma wafting towards Cabrakan 's nostrils – mmm, mmmh! He drooled, he dribbled, the saliva trickled from the corners of his mouth.

'Give me some,' he said.

'Of course, friend,' replied the twins. 'Here is one we cooked earlier, especially for you.' And they handed the giant a bird completely encased in a coating of baked mud. Being ignorant of culinary matters – and by now very hungry – Cabrakan did not notice that this was different from the other birds on the spit. He grabbed it and gobbled it up in its entirety, flesh, bones, mud and all.

'That's better!' he said, rubbing his capacious belly and then letting out a satisfied belch.

The trio continued on their way. Cabrakan, however, found himself becoming unusually and unaccountably tired. Each and every step demanded increasing effort. He felt so heavy, dragged down as if by a great weight inside him. The enchanted bird he had eaten was doing its work.

Succumbing to irresistible weariness and exhaustion, he was finally overcome and sank to the ground. The twins bound him, bending his arms and legs into the foetal position so that his body was a ball. They buried him there in the east, opposite his brother in the west, heaping the earth up over the dead giant just as they had heaped earth around the bird he had eaten.

Cabrakan, the last of the line of Seven Macaw, was dead.

Hunahpu and Xbalanque, the monster-slayers, went on to have other adventures in which they met and defeated other demons, other cosmic agents of destruction. And all of this they did out of the pureness of their hearts, to prepare the world for a coming race – a people whom the gods would make from a paste of cornmeal and water. Humankind.

The Black Road to Xibalba

• MAYA •

THEY STILL STAND, the ballcourts of the Maya lords: two stone walls flanking a broad alley, a replica in miniature of the face of the world. On this world-plain, a cosmic game of chance was once enacted. Here men played ball for their lives. Their invisible adversary was Death. When the game was done and Death departed, he was never alone.

The tale that unfolds before you now concerns a pair of twins who were called to play ball with the Lords of Death. Named after days in the sacred calendar, they were Hun Hunahpu and Vucub Hunahpu – One Hunahpu and Seven Hunahpu. They were the sons of Xmucane, the divine Grandmother who could read the auguries of the days.

One Hunahpu had a wife called Egret Woman and together they also produced twins, Hun Batz and Hun Chouen – One Monkey and One Artisan. Named like their father and uncle after days in the calendar, the boys grew to be skilled in all the arts. They played the flute, they sang, they wrote, they worked in jade and precious metals.

While One Monkey and One Artisan were engaged in their creative endeavours, One Hunahpu and Seven Hunahpu went down to the ballcourt to hone their skills. All day, every day they practised, in their court in the east, until they had become the finest ballplayers in all the world.

Sometimes One Monkey and One Artisan would join them in a game, making up a foursome with two to a side. Watched by the falcon, messenger of Hurricane, Heart of Heaven, they moved rapidly up and down the ballcourt, bouncing the ball – a sphere of solid rubber more than a handspan wide – off their torsos, their arms, their shoulders, their thighs, never touching it with their hands, as they tried to propel it through one of the hoops in the court's sloping walls. It was a game of skill and speed and, since the body itself served as a bat, it was also one which could lead to injury. To prevent this, the players wore protective yokes around their waists, guards around their arms and kilts around their thighs. What sport they had, what excitement!

Now it was the day called Hunahpu and Venus the Morning Star appeared in the east, over the teams at play on their ballcourt. It was a particularly fast and noisy game. *Bounce, bump, thump.* The ball thudded against stone and bone and flesh.

Bounce, bump, thump. The sound drummed through the soil beneath their feet and reverberated through the underworld of Xibalba, where it rattled the composure of the Lords of Death.

'Who is this who stamps above our heads? Who is this who disturbs our peace? Let them come here to pit their skills against us!' roared the Death Lords and they sent their messenger owls to fetch them.

'We will go,' said One Hunahpu and Seven Hunahpu. 'You – One Monkey and One Artisan – you stay here, to comfort and amuse your grandmother.' And to a tearful Xmucane they said, 'It is only a game, Mother – we are not going to die.'

Then the spear-like Shooting Owl, the One-legged Owl, the red-backed Macaw Owl and the legless Skull Owl all led them away.

Following their guides, the brothers walked over the eastern rim of the world. They passed through roaring canyons and caves, through rapids flowing with scorpions, over a river of blood, across a river of pus and yet they survived all these hazards. But then they came to a crossroads where four paths met. Which should they take: Red, Black, White or Yellow? East, West, North or South?

'Take me,' the Black Road of the West whispered treacherously, 'I am the path you must follow.' So the brothers placed their feet on the Black Road and their fate was sealed. This was the road of no return, which begins where the Milky Way parts and plummets behind the eastern horizon, leading westwards into the realm of Death. It was Qeqa Be, the Black Road of Xibalba.

Down in Xibalba, the Lords were waiting. Chief among them were Hun Kame, One Death, and Vucub Kame, Seven Death. In the lower ranks were every demon, every malevolent spirit, every agent of sickness and misery whom you could possibly imagine. There were Scab Picker and Blood Taker, who stripped the scabs off men's skins and collected their blood. There were the Demons of Pus and of Jaundice, whose pleasure it was to make humans swell, to afflict them with suppurating sores, to turn their skins yellow. Next in rank were Bone Sceptre and Skull Sceptre, who inflicted the chosen with dropsy or skeletal emaciation. The Demon of Filth and the Demon of Sorrow, drawn to dirt on the threshold like flies to rotting meat left, as their parting gifts, sudden shock and death. And Wing and Packstrap roamed the open road looking for their victims, who died vomiting blood.

This was the cheerful company who waited for One and Seven Hunahpu. Practical jokers all, with a sense of humour as black as the Black Road, they could not suppress their excitement.

One Hunahpu and Seven Hunahpu entered the meeting place of Xibalba, where the Lords held council. Seated there was a row of figures.

'Greetings, Your Lordships, One Death and Seven Death,' the newcomers said to the first and second. The figures made no answer. They neither moved nor responded; they were as stiff as wood. But how could it be otherwise when they were made from wood? The figures were nothing but mannikins, put there to deceive. And how the brothers had been deceived! How easily they had fallen into the trap! The real Lords of Xibalba, released from their faked immobility, laughed until their sides ached, their skulls rattled, their blood gurgled and their sores burst.

'Welcome,' said One Death and Seven Death. 'You will, I am sure, excuse our little jest. Tomorrow you will play in the ballcourt. But for now you must rest. Please be seated, here on this stone bench.'

One Hunahpu and Seven Hunahpu lowered themselves on to the stone, but leapt up again immediately, clutching their buttocks and howling with pain. The stone was as burning hot as a griddle. If they had sat on it any longer, they would have been well and truly cooked. Oh, it was too much! How the Lords of Death and Disease screamed with laughter! They rolled on the ground, they shrieked, they sobbed. They laughed until the sound rose up through

the roof of Xibalba and shook the world above. This was an even better joke than the last one!

But now the time for humour was past. It was time to be serious. The Lords proposed to ensnare One and Seven Hunahpu with a devious and deadly trick.

In Xibalba there were several houses of ordeal and in one of them the brothers must spend the night. Which one should the Lords choose? There was Rattling House, which shook with draughts and clattered with hail and was cold as ice inside. There was Jaguar House, in which the big cats, growling, ravenous and ceaselessly prowling, were confined. There was Bat House, where bats darted blindly about, emitting their high-pitched squeaks as they banged against the walls of their prison. There was Cutting House, in which blades, moving back and forth with the swing of a pendulum, sliced and slivered the space inside. Or there was Dark House, which was filled with nothing but the densest and most palpable blackness. This was the place that the Lords settled on as sleeping quarters for their guests.

The brothers were conducted there. The darkness enveloped them like a thick blanket and their hearts were filled with fear.

'Take these,' said a bearer sent by One and Seven Death and he handed them a torch and two cigars. 'The torch will give you light and the cigars will help you while away the night. But remember that these things do not belong to you. In the morning you must give them back in the same condition as you received them – whole.'

This, of course, was impossible. Once the torch was lit, the greedy flame consumed the fibre until only a stump remained. The cigars burned sweetly for a time, scenting the interior with their smoke. But then they too, reduced to blackened stubs, died, leaving One and Seven Hunahpu alone in the darkness.

'Where is our torch? Our cigars?' asked One and Seven Death when the brothers came before them the next day.

'Forgive us, your Lordships. We have used them all up.'

'What is this? Used them all up? Did we not *tell* you, in the plainest possible terms, that you were to return them whole? A simple enough request, surely? And yet you stand here empty-handed! No, we are not going to waste time playing ball with the likes of you. There is only one option – you must die!'

This was the best joke of all.

The brothers were led out to the altar of sacrifice, where defeated ballplayers were killed. There they were sacrificed and buried side by side, together in death as they had been in life. The head of One Hunahpu was not interred with his body, however. After he was killed, it was cut off and placed in the fork of a tree, from which it gazed glumly at its surroundings.

As the two brothers were lowered into the ground, Venus the Evening Star sank in the west and the day was called Death.

The tree stood silent and barren. The only fruit it bore was the skull of One Hunahpu. And then something strange and miraculous happened. Nodules appeared on its branches. They swelled and grew into fat, round gourds. For the first time in its life the tree had fruited and the fruits it bore were calabashes. They smothered the branches and were as like as peas in a pod to the skull of One Hunahpu, still wedged in the fork.

This new development perturbed the Lords of Xibalba. They came to look at the magical tree. There were mutterings of sorcery and dark doings.

'This tree is out of bounds,' decreed One Death and Seven Death. 'No one is to come near it.'

But someone did – the maiden Xkik, Blood Moon, daughter of Blood Taker, the Xibalban Lord of the fourth rank. Having heard of the wonderful calabash tree, Blood Moon had to see for herself. She went there, secretly and alone. She marvelled at the laden branches with their rich harvest, just begging to be picked.

'What a waste', she thought, 'if no one gathers this fruit, if it is left to wither on the stalk.' And she reached out for one of the calabashes, the one wedged in the tree.

'Why do you want a round, bony thing like me?' said the calabash, which was really a skull.

'Oh, but I do!' said the maiden.

'Then show me,' said the skull. 'Bring your hand closer, here where I can see it.'

Blood Moon stretched out her right hand as far as she could. *Phut!* The skull spat a gobbet of saliva straight into the maiden's palm. But when she examined it a second

later her palm was quite dry. At that moment something began to grow in her belly.

As the months passed Blood Moon's belly swelled, like the virgin Moon as she waxes and fattens.

'You have been with a man!' shouted Blood Taker, as the evidence of his daughter's pregnancy grew increasingly impossible to ignore. 'Who is the father of the child you carry? I demand to know. Tell me or you shall die!'

'There is no father, my lord, no man whose face or flesh I know.'

This, of course, was quite true, but it enraged Blood Taker.

'Lie to me, will you? Well, you know the punishment for deceit!' And he ordered the owls of Xibalba to take his daughter away and kill her and bring her heart back to him in a bowl.

The owls led the princess away, taking with them also the white dagger of sacrifice. But Blood Moon talked to them and reasoned with them, insisting on her innocence, until at last they were persuaded and agreed not to kill her.

'But what shall we use for a heart?' they asked.

'Use the sap of the croton tree,' said the princess. And when the tree was tapped it bled a sap as red as blood. The sap congealed in the bowl and Blood Moon rolled it into a ball, crusted and wet on the outside, with all the appearance of a real heart. 'Take that to your masters,' she said.

The Lords of Xibalba placed the fake heart on the sacrificial fire. *Mmm, mm.* The smoke was sweet, so sweet. They breathed it in, deeply and appreciatively. Who could have guessed that a maiden's heart would smell so good?

That was how Blood Moon deceived the Lords of Death. Never again would they receive human hearts in sacrifice. Instead they would be given lumps of croton sap burned as incense.

Blood Moon, meanwhile, escaped from Xibalba through a hole in the Earth which the owls had shown her. She made straight for the home of Xmucane.

'Good-day, Grandmother. I am your daughter. I bear in my belly the children of your sons.' By now Blood Moon knew the full truth. The saliva of the skull in the calabash tree which had caused her pregnancy contained the seed not just of One Hunahpu but also of his brother Seven Hunahpu. And it was not one child but two that she carried.

'You lie! My sons are dead!' cried Xmucane.

'No, Grandmother, they are not dead. You shall see their faces again in the faces of your grandchildren.'

'Very well, then, if you are truly who you say, go and gather food for your children. Gather a netful of ripe ears of corn and bring it back here to me.'

Blood Moon went out to the garden which One Monkey and One Artisan had planted, but all she saw there was a single maize plant bearing a single ear of corn. All around, the rest of the garden was bare. So she raised her voice and began to sing a song, invoking the goddess who guarded the crops in the garden. 'Come Thunder Woman, Yellow Woman, Cacao Woman, Cornmeal Woman – arise,' she chanted, using all of the goddess's names. Then she took hold of the silken tassels of the plant and began to pull. And as she pulled the magic started to work. The silken tassels were like a gushing spring, spewing out cob after fat cob, and in no time at all her net was full to overflowing.

'Hmph,' said a sceptical Xmucane when she saw Blood Moon's harvest. 'Where did all that come from? You must have stripped the entire garden! Well, I'm going to see for myself!' And she stamped off to check on Blood Moon's work. But when she arrived at the plot, there stood the single maize plant, just as before, and all around it the soil was smooth and undisturbed. At the foot of the plant was the imprint of a net. Xmucane knew that this was a sign and the sign told her the truth.

She returned to Blood Moon and acknowledged her as her daughter-in-law. And as Venus the Morning Star appeared in the east, Blood Moon gave birth to twin boys. Their names were Hunahpu and Xbalanque and the day was called Net.

A great destiny awaited the boys. They would go where their fathers had gone, they would succeed where their fathers had failed and they would go some way to vanquishing the dark powers of Xibalba. But all that, of course, is another story.

THE BALLGAME

The ballgame which features prominently in the stories of the two pairs of divine twins – One Hunahpu and Seven Hunahpu, and Hunahpu and Xbalanque – was played all over Mesoamerica and is still played in north-western Mexico.

Special courts were built for it consisting of an alley flanked on either side by parallel sloping walls. Sometimes additional sections ran at right angles across the top and bottom of the alley, creating an I-shaped layout.

The balls used were made of solid rubber from the sap of the rubber tree, *Castilla elastica*, which grew locally, and were dense and heavy. Those used in the modern game measure 10 cm (4 in) across and weigh about 500 g (1 lb); those used by the Maya may have been as much as 30–45 cm (12–18 in) wide and weighed around 3.5 kg (8 lb), which almost makes them offensive weapons! As a macabre alternative, hollow balls may have been produced by encasing the skulls of defeated players in rubber.

The game was played by two teams each with two or three members. The aim was to propel the ball through rings, known as markers, which protruded from the court's walls. This cannot have been easy because, other than at the start of the game when they threw it into play, players were not allowed to touch the ball with their hands. Instead, they had to use their bodies as bats deflecting the ball off their torsos, arms and thighs.

Protective equipment included heavy padding around the knees, waists and arms and, among the Maya, distinctive horseshoe-shaped yokes worn around the waist. Stone yokes have survived, but since these weigh around 13.5 kg (30 lb) they are more likely to have been trophies or ceremonial items. The yokes used in play were made of wicker or reed fibre. Decoratively carved stone objects known as *hachas* and *palmas* may have been inserted into them to deflect the ball and protect the body further.

The Mesoamerican ballgame involved heavy gambling, but also had great symbolic meaning. It was a cosmic metaphor for the movements of the heavenly bodies, notably the Sun, Moon and Venus. It was also a re-enactment of war in which defeated players were sometimes decapitated – skullracks known as *tzompantli* have been found next to ballcourts (the severed head of One Hunahpu in the calabash tree alludes to one such rack). In a Maya ritual, war captives were trussed up to provide a human 'ball' and bounced down a flight of steps adjacent to the ballcourt (like the sacrificial victims thrown down the temple steps by the Aztecs). And finally, the Mesoamerican ballgame symbolized the game of life and death itself.

At Play on the Ballcourt of Death

• MAYA •

Do you know the story of One Hunahpu and Seven Hunahpu, sons of Grandmother Xmucane, who set off on the Black Road to Xibalba but were never seen again? Do you know of the maiden Blood Moon, a princess of Xibalba, who bore them two sons on a day called Net, as Venus the Morning Star appeared in the east?

This is the story of those children, the twin sons of Blood Moon. Their names are Hunahpu and Xbalanque.

Born in the mountains, Hunahpu and Xbalanque were wild and noisy.

'I can't stand it!' cried Grandmother Xmucane. 'These children are too rowdy. I will not let them stay in my house. Send them outside!'

So the twins had to live in the open. They slept on anthills and in brambles, yet they remained unharmed – a fact which did not please One Monkey and One Artisan, the boys' twin half-brothers. These two nourished a private jealousy of their younger siblings. They had hoped that the ants would bite them to death, that the brambles would tear their skin and were highly disappointed when they did not.

Each day Hunahpu and Xbalanque went hunting and brought back birds for the pot. But they received little thanks for their efforts, and even less love, from either Xmucane or their half-brothers. When they came for their meals, they found that One Monkey and One Artisan had already eaten their share. While they were out hunting to provide food for their family, all their half-brothers did was to sit in the sun and strum and sing. This state of affairs continued for a time and then, one day, Hunahpu and Xbalanque returned home empty-handed.

'Why have you brought me no birds? What are we going to eat?' demanded Grandmother Xmucane.

'We have plenty of birds, dear Grandmother,' the twins replied, 'but they are stuck in the tree. Please ask our brothers to help get them down.'

Reluctantly and with an ill grace One Monkey and One Artisan followed the twins to the tree and there, on every branch, were birds with every imaginable feather, twittering, chirping and screeching – more than a hunter could ever hope to see gathered in one place.

Hunahpu and Xbalanque began blowing their darts, but although these found their mark, the birds did not fall from the tree but remained suspended in its branches.

'You must climb up and get them,' said the twins to their half-brothers.

As One Monkey and One Artisan clambered up the trunk, something strange started to happen. Could they be imagining it? The tree seemed to be getting taller. The higher they went, the further they had to go. It was impossible, it could not be! It was as if the tree were deliberately stretching away from them to prevent them reaching its upper branches. They would be carried off, up into the clouds. Looking up made them giddy, looking down made them ill – the ground seemed to be a dizzying distance away.

'Help!' they called faintly from their eyrie. 'We can't get down. What shall we do?'

'In situations such as these', cooed their brothers from below, 'the first rule is: don't panic. Do exactly as we tell you. Undo your loincloths and tie them around your waist so that the ends are hanging down like tails behind you. Then you'll be freer to move.'

One Monkey and One Artisan did exactly as instructed. And it was true, they did find it easier to move unrestricted by clothing – but then monkeys have no need of clothing. For that is what the pair had become, up there in the branches. And there the simian brothers stayed, chattering and howling and swinging their loincloth-tails as they leapt from tree to tree.

'Grandmother,' said Hunahpu and Xbalanque on returning home, 'something terrible has happened. Our brothers are behaving like animals and won't come down from the tree. But don't be sad – we will get them back for you. Only you must promise not to laugh.' And they began to drum and sing and play a tune called Hunahpu Monkey.

It was irresistible. One Monkey and One Artisan came scuttling out of the forest, dancing and twirling a-tiptoe and tumbling like acrobats. Seeing their strange antics, their ugly, scrunched-up faces and their skinny little genitals dangling between their legs, Xmucane – try as she might – could not contain her laughter. She laughed until her belly shook and her mouth ached. Her laughter drove One Monkey and One Artisan back into the trees.

'Grandmother!' Hunahpu and Xbalanque rebuked her gently. 'We did ask you not to laugh. Now *please* – let's try again.'

Taking up their instruments once more, they began to play and sing. As before, One Monkey and One Artisan came tripping out of the forest, unable to resist the foot-tapping music. As before, Xmucane was unable to keep silent and again her laughter sent her monkey grandsons back into the forest.

Hunahpu and Xbalanque made two more attempts – which, of course, they knew would fail.

'Never mind,' they said to Xmucane. 'You have us and our mother. Love us and all will be well.' And so matters were resolved between the Grandmother and her grandsons.

As for One Monkey and One Artisan, they stayed in the forest for the rest of their lives and were much revered by musicians and singers.

It will be seen from this episode that Hunahpu and Xbalanque were young men with very special qualities and the time was coming for them to fulfil their destiny.

One day they informed their mother and grandmother that they were going out to clear some land and create a garden. They took with them a mattock, a hoe and an axe. But the grind of physical toil was not for beings such as they. Placing the mattock and hoe in the soil and the axe in the trunk of a tree, they sat back and waited. Obligingly, the tools jumped into action.

Tock, tock went the mattock as it broke up the earth.

Snip, snip went the hoe as it sliced through the weeds.

Chop, chop went the axe as it cut down the trees.

Coo, coo went the dove as it warned of the approach of Xmucane, bringing their meal.

Quickly the brothers grabbed the tools to still them. Then one rubbed dirt over his hands and face, while the other worked wood dust into his hair. Now they looked their parts – a real gardener and a real woodcutter.

'Food – just what we need!' they chorused as Xmucane appeared. 'We're exhausted! We couldn't have dug and chopped for another second.'

That night at home they continued their play-acting, making a great show of stretching and rubbing their arms and legs.

'Aah,' they sighed. 'That's better. We ache all over from working so hard.' Mother and Grandmother were totally deceived.

The next day Hunahpu and Xbalanque returned to the plot they – or rather their tools – had cleared, to begin planting. But what did they see? A forest of trees, a jungle of vegetation. All the previous day's labour was undone. Some magic must be at work here. After putting their mattock and hoe and axe into action again, the brothers decided to keep watch overnight.

At midnight, concealed in the bushes by the side of the plot, they heard a rustle and a padding and scampering of soft feet and, as they watched, they saw the puma and the jaguar enter the clearing. Next came the deer and the rabbit, the fox and coyote, the hog, raccoon and rat. Sitting in the middle of the space, the animals began a hypnotic chant: 'Come, trees, come. Come, bushes, come. Sprout and bud and burgeon out. Come, plants, come.'

As the words floated out on the midnight air, shoots and saplings, called up by magic, began to grow and proliferate. The animals stood up and started to leave. Hunahpu and Xbalanque tried to catch them as they passed, but all they managed to grab were the tails of the deer and the rabbit, which came off in their hands (which is why the deer and the rabbit still have stumps for tails).

The last creature to leave the clearing was the rat. Deftly the brothers blocked his exit and threw a net over him.

'You, rat!' they shouted. 'Why do you want to destroy our work?' And in a fit of revenge they tried to choke him, and they held him over their fire so that all the hair on his tail was burned off (which is why the rat still has a hairless tail).

'Please don't kill me!' the rat cried. 'You are not gardeners, you are not farmers! Your destiny lies elsewhere. I hold the secret inside me. Free me and give me my food and I will tell you what it is.'

'Very well,' said Hunahpu and Xbalanque, removing the net. 'Speak!'

'Hidden beneath the rafters of your grandmother's house is something that belonged to your fathers, One Hunahpu and Seven Hunahpu, who died at the hands of the Lords of Death. It is the ball and yokes and armguards which they once used in their games on their ballcourt in the east. Retrieve these things and they will lead you on the path of destiny.'

The brothers were overjoyed. 'Corn kernels, squash seeds, beans, chilli peppers, cocoa beans – these belong to you,' they said, as they named the rat's foods. Then they returned home, taking the rat with them. They said nothing of what they had learned to their grandmother and hid the rat in the roof.

'Grandmother,' they said. 'We have a yearning for one of your chilli stews. Please would you make some for us?'

When the stew was set before them, they created a diversion to occupy their mother and grandmother. They sent a mosquito to puncture the side of the water container so that the women, busied outside in trying to stop up the hole and refill the vessel, would not notice the sounds of gnawing above. Chewing away with his sharp teeth, the rat was working to release the ties that held the ball, the yokes and the guards. The brothers could see him, reflected in the glistening chilli sauce.

At last all the equipment came tumbling down. Hunahpu and Xbalanque took it to the old ballcourt in the east, unused for so long.

They swept and tidied the court, and then they began to play as if born to it. Moving fast and furiously up and down the alley, they bounced the ball off their torsos, their arms, their shoulders, their thighs, never touching it with their hands, as they attempted to propel it through one of the hoops in the sloping walls. What sport they had, what excitement!

Bounce, bump, thump. The ball thudded against stone and bone and flesh. *Bounce, bump, thump.* The sound drummed through the soil beneath their feet and reverberated through the underworld of Xibalba, where it rattled the composure of the Lords of Death.

'Who is this who stamps above our heads? Who is this who disturbs our peace? Let them come here to pit their skills against us!' roared the Death Lords, and they sent their messenger owls to fetch them.

Grandmother Xmucane was all alone when the owls arrived. She sobbed when she heard their words. 'Am I to lose my grandsons as well as my sons?' she asked. But this was an invitation that could not be refused, so she sent a louse to take the owls' message to Hunahpu and Xbalanque.

'Tell them this,' she said to the little creature that she held in her palm. 'In seven days they must go to Xibalba, to play on the ballcourt of Death.'

The louse set off. On the way he met a toad.

'Good-day, Brother Louse,' said the toad. 'Where are you going and what is your errand?'

'I am going to Hunahpu and Xbalanque with a secret message. I hold the secret inside me.'

'But you are so slow! If you allow me to swallow you, we will get there all the faster.'

The louse agreed. The toad swallowed him and went hopping along the road.

Presently the toad met a snake.

'Good-day, Brother Toad. Where are you going and what is your errand?'

'I am going to Hunahpu and Xbalanque with a secret message. I hold the secret inside me.'

'Let me swallow you and we'll get there all the faster.'

The toad agreed. The snake swallowed him and went slithering along the road.

Presently the snake noticed a falcon, hovering above him.

'Good-day, Brother Snake. Where are you going and what is your errand?'

'I am going to Hunahpu and Xbalanque with a secret message. I hold the secret inside me.'

'Let me swallow you and we'll get there all the faster.'

The snake agreed. The falcon swallowed him and went swooping along over the road and alighted by the side of the ballcourt, where Hunahpu and Xbalanque were playing. 'Wuk-oh, wuk-oh,' he cried, in his strange, laughing call.

'Who is that? Who is there?' shouted the brothers and – practised hunters that they were – they raised their blowgun and blew their dart right in the falcon's eye. The wounded bird fell to the ground.

'What do you want?' said the brothers.

'I have a secret message for you. I hold the secret inside me. Heal my eye first and I'll let the secret out.'

Hunahpu and Xbalanque took a piece of rubber from the ball and used this to stop up the wound in the falcon's eye (which is why this particular bird still has a black patch around his eye). 'Now spit it out!' they said.

The falcon spat out the snake.

The snake spat out the toad.

The toad spat out the louse.

And the louse spoke: 'I have a message from your grandmother. She says that in seven days you must go to Xibalba to play on the ballcourt of Death.'

Hunahpu and Xbalanque went at once to Xmucane and Blood Moon, their mother.

'Dear Mother and Grandmother, we are leaving,' they told them. 'But we will leave you a sign. Here are two ears of green corn. We will leave them in the rafters. Guard them well, for they contain the living spirit of the corn. When the corn in the field ripens and dries, you will know we are dead. When it grows again, then you will know that we live.'

And so saying they left, taking their blowgun with them.

Down the eastern slope of the world they descended, just as One and Seven Hunahpu, their fathers, had done. They passed safely through the canyons, over the scorpion rapids and the rivers of pus and blood, and then they came to the crossing of the four roads, Red, Black, White, and Yellow, and now, in the middle, there was another of Green, the road of beauty, the path which all wish to walk.

Hunahu and Xbalanque were cleverer than their fathers before them, for they knew that the Lords of Death were waiting to trick them. They would match them with tricks of their own. So they called the mosquito to them. 'Sister Mosquito,' they said, 'go before us and bite the Lords of Xibalba. Do this and yours alone will be the blood of travellers on the road.'

How could the mosquito refuse? She darted off at once, ahead of the brothers, to the meeting place where the Lords held council. There they all sat, the Princes of Death and the Demons of Disease, ranged by their rank, waiting.

The mosquito sunk her sharp, piercing mouthparts into the flesh of the first. There was no response. She moved on to the second. Silence. She bit the third. 'Ow!' She had hit flesh and blood. The first two figures were wooden mannikins, put there to deceive.

This was One Death himself.

The mosquito passed on down the ranks. 'Ow!' cried Seven Death. 'Ow!' cried Scab Picker and Blood Taker and the Demon of Pus and the Demon of Jaundice, Bone Sceptre and Skull Sceptre and the Demon of Filth and the Demon of Sorrow and Wing and Packstrap and all the others as she bit them each in turn. And as each cried out, his neighbour would ask, 'What is the matter, Scab Picker?' – or Blood Taker or whatever his name happened to be. And so Hunahpu and Xbalanque were able to sort wood from flesh and addressed all the Lords by their correct names when they entered Xibalba on the day called Hunahpu, as Venus the Evening Star sank in the west.

'Please be seated,' said One and Seven Death to their visitors, indicating the red-hot stone slab.

'That is no bench – that's a hot stone for cooking! We'll not be seated there,' replied the brothers as they refused the Lords' invitation.

That night they were conducted to the House of Darkness, where – like their fathers before them – they were given the torch and the cigars, which they were to burn but return whole in the morning. Again they outwitted their hosts. They replaced the flames on the torch with macaw feathers and the sparks on the ends of the cigars with fireflies. Consequently, when they came before the Lords again the following day, the torch and cigars were as good as new.

'Let's play!' said the Lords and they brought out their ball – a round, pale object the colour of bone.

'That's no ball – that's a skull!' said the twins.

'Nonsense, dear boys! Its decoration is deceptive. It only *looks* like a skull.'

Play began as Venus the Evening Star watched from the west.

The Lords batted the bone-ball one way, the twins another. Suddenly, Hunahpu's yoke caught it and deflected it downwards. It fell to the ground and broke open and the white dagger of sacrifice slithered out. The dagger snaked across the ballcourt, twisting and turning and pricking at the brothers' flesh as it tried to stab them. But Hunahpu and Xbalanque, agile as athletes, escaped.

'What kind of hosts are you?' the brothers demanded of the Lords of Xibalba. 'Do you invite us here only to kill us? Where is your sporting spirit?' And they made as if to leave.

'No, no. Please stay,' protested the Lords, for without the brothers they would be deprived of their amusement.

The twins' own rubber ball was then brought out. 'What prize will you have if you win? Name it!' they said to the Lords.

'Flowers – we want flowers. Four bowls of them – red petals, white petals, yellow petals and whole blooms.' And so it was agreed. Deep in their hearts, the Lords were jubilant. Where on earth, or indeed under it, were their opponents to find flowers? This time, they felt, they had won. And indeed, when play resumed, the brothers lost.

That night, to reinforce their defeat, the Lords sent them to Cutting House, where blades, moving back and forth with the swing of a pendulum, sliced and slivered the space inside. Here, their hosts hoped, the knives would do their work. But they did not. Instead, they heard Hunahpu and Xbalanque whispering to them: 'Spare us, and the flesh of animals will be yours to cut.' How could the knives refuse? They at once grew still.

Then the brothers summoned the leafcutter ants. 'Sister ants, come. Fetch us the flowers of Xibalba, from the garden of One and Seven Death.'

The ants streamed into the garden and swarmed across the soil, up plant stems, up tree trunks. They bit and nibbled and chewed and took flower after flower in their stout little mandibles, which they brought to Hunahpu and Xbalanque. Then they returned for more.

'Whippoorwill-poorwill,' sang the nightjars set to guard the garden.

'What a fine night it is,' said one.

'Indeed,' said the other, oblivious as they both were to the activity around them, even when the ends of their own tails and wing feathers were nibbled off.

As the columns of busy ants went to and fro, it was as if the entire garden was on the move and all the flowers had sprouted legs. Red, white and yellow, petals and blossom of every shape and size – they piled into the bowls like showers of confetti and soon filled each to the brim.

When the Lords of Xibalba received their tribute in the morning, they were amazed. When they learned where the flowers had come from, their amazement turned to outrage. They went pale. They felt sick. What kind of people were these brothers? So far, the Lords had been outwitted at every turn.

'Why were you not watching?' they raged at the bird guardians. 'How could you let them do this?' And in punishment for their lack of attention, they split the birds' mouths wide open (which is why whippoorwills and poorwills still have wide gapes).

The following night, after a game which ended in a draw, the Lords sent Hunahpu and Xbalanque to Rattling House, which shook with draughts and clattered with hail and was cold as ice inside. There they shivered away the dark hours, but at dawn they were still alive.

'How do they do it?' the Lords wondered, and play resumed again.

The next night they sent them to Jaguar House, in which the big cats, growling, ravenous and ceaselessly prowling, were confined. Here, the Lords thought, the jaguars would make a quick meal of the brothers. But they did not. Instead they heard Hunahpu and Xbalanque whispering, 'Don't eat us – eat these instead,' as they threw a handful of bones before them.

The jaguars fought over the bones, then settled down to a purring feast. 'Ah!' said the satisfied sentries, peering in. 'They will never see the ballcourt again! Just look at them – they are nothing but skeletons.' But at dawn the twins stepped out with barely a scratch on them.

The Lords of Xibalba could hardly believe their eyes, and play resumed again.

The next night they sent them to Fire House. Although the flames licked around the twins, they did not burn them, but just kept them toasting warm, and at dawn they stepped out with barely a scorch mark on them.

The Lords of Xibalba were beginning to lose heart. Was it possible for two men to be invincible? Play resumed again.

That night the Lords sent them to Bat House, where bats darted blindly about, emitting their high-pitched squeaks as they banged against the walls of their prison. For safety the twins hid in their blowgun.

When the bats quietened down as if preparing for their daytime sleep, Xbalanque spoke. 'Is it dawn yet, Brother?' he asked. Hunahpu poked out his head to take a look. But as he did so, one of the bats swooped down and snapped his head off.

'Speak to me, Brother!' said Xbalanque. 'What do you see?' But the body of Hunahpu, which was still stuffed inside the blowgun, had no lips with which to answer. For the first time in Xibalba, Xbalanque felt the pricking of despair.

Bump, bump, bump – the severed head bounced out of Bat House and rolled on to the ballcourt, much to the delight of the Lords of Xibalba. Now this was more like it! A human head was much more fun to play with than a rubber ball – better still, it was the head of Hunahpu. They had won at last!

Xbalanque, meanwhile, called all the animals to him. He told them to bring him their belongings, so that he could see what he might see. One brought wood, another leaves, another stones, another earth. Last of all, trailing after the others, came the raccoon, pushing a pumpkin along with his snout.

Xbalanque took the pumpkin and carved a face on it. Then Hurricane, Heart of Heaven, came down from the sky and placed a brain where pith and seeds had been. And as Old Man Possum was drawing streaks of red and blue across the dawn sky, Xbalanque planted the pumpkin head firmly on Hunahpu's shoulders.

'Good-day, Brother,' it said.

Finally, Xbalanque instructed the rabbit: 'Hide among the ball bags at the top of the court … and when the ball comes in your direction – run!'

Then, as Venus the Evening Star watched from the west, Xbalanque went to play ball on the ballcourt of Death.

On the court the Lords were waiting, the scent of victory in their nostrils. Play began. The Lords sent Hunahpu's head spinning. Xbalanque intercepted it. He hit it with all his force. The head went soaring up into the air and came down with a bump among the ball bags, where the rabbit was waiting. The rabbit sprang up and began bouncing away, with the entire company of the Lords of Xibalba in shrill and shrieking pursuit.

That left the court clear for Xbalanque.

Picking up his brother's real head, he swapped it for the pumpkin. Hunahpu now had his own head back and the pumpkin lay on the ballcourt.

'Come back!' cried Xbalanque. 'I've found the ball.'

When the Xibalbans returned, puffing and panting from their wild rabbit chase, they were amazed to see not one, but two brothers on the court.

Play resumed in earnest. The pumpkin was knocked hither and thither around the ballcourt until at last its soft rind burst, spattering the Lords with flesh and seeds.

They knew that they had been taken for fools.

Hunahpu and Xbalanque had survived all the tricks and traps that the Lords of Xibalba had set before them – roaring canyons, rapids running with scorpions, rivers of blood and pus, wooden dolls, a burning stone slab, houses filled with darkness, cold, knives, fire, jaguars and bats. And, above all, they had survived the ballgame itself.

The Lords would not take kindly to such humiliation. Hunahpu and Xbalanque knew that this time they would be killed. So they visited two seers called Xulu and Pacam.

'The Lords of Xibalba are plotting our death,' they said. 'This is what you must say when they ask you how to dispose of our remains.' And they whispered the secret in their ears.

Meanwhile, the Lords were preparing for the most satisfying sacrifice they had received in a long while. But, addicted as they were to practical jokes, they were unable to conduct even this ceremony without trickery and subterfuge.

'Come,' they said to Hunahpu and Xbalanque, 'see what we have made for you,' and they indicated a great stone pit in which, they claimed, they were brewing an intoxicating liquor. In truth, the pit was an oven of death. 'Come, let's jump over it,' they said.

But Hunahpu and Xbalanque had had enough of jokes. Taking each other's hands, they jumped – not across the pit, but into it – and in an instant were devoured by the flames. Just as the brothers had predicted, the Lords then consulted Xulu and Pacam as to the means of their disposal.

'Shall we throw their bones in the canyon?'

'No. They would come back to life.'

'Hang them up in a tree?'

'No. You would still see their faces.'

BLOOD AND HUMAN SACRIFICE

For Mesoamerican peoples, blood was the essence of life, the substance which fuelled the turning of the world. Human blood and human life were the greatest gifts they could give to the gods who had made them and to whom they owed an eternal debt. In return for this gift of life, the gods expected humans to provide them with sustenance. In Maya myth, Tohil, god of the Quiché Maya, openly demanded human sacrifice. The Aztec gods had given their blood to make the first humans, and had given their lives so that the Sun would move across the sky – their worshippers could hardly do less. Knowing that blood was the food of gods, the Aztecs sent *tamales* (maize cakes) soaked in blood to the *conquistador* Cortés when he arrived on Mexican soil.

The aristocratic ritual of bloodletting was one way of paying humanity's blood debt to the gods. Various parts of the body were bled, including the shins, knees, elbows, earlobes, tongues and penises. Stingray spines, flint, bone or obsidian lancets and, in central Mexico, maguey spines were all used for this. According to Maya art, the flowing blood ran along cords passed through the wounds on to strips of paper in wide bowls. The blood-soaked paper was then burnt, and in the rising column of smoke, the penitents – hallucinating through loss of blood – might see the rearing Vision Serpent and the face of the deity or ancestor to whom the gift of blood had been made.

Of all Mesoamerican peoples, the Aztecs are most strongly associated with human sacrifice, if only because of the vast numbers of victims said to be involved. According to Spanish observers, they sacrificed between 20,000 and 50,000 people a year in Tenochtitlán, their capital. Such excess seems to have been a symptom of near-panic that, without offerings on this scale, the gods would turn their backs on the human race.

The favoured victims were war captives. When there were too few, the Aztecs fought ceremonial battles with their neighbours, in which both sides would take captives purely for the purpose of sacrifice. Their senses dulled by narcotic plants, the victims had their hearts removed – a quick death, apparently, and one which brought great honour. Heart sacrifice was also practised among the Toltecs, while the Maya often decapitated their victims.

Further to the south, the Incas practised human sacrifice, too. One notable and particularly poignant custom was the rite known as *capacocha*, in which the victims were usually children. After going to Cuzco to be blessed by the Inca priests, the *capacochas* returned home, in procession along straight routes called *ceques*. Here they were either buried alive in subterranean tombs or killed with clubs and their bodies left on mountaintops.

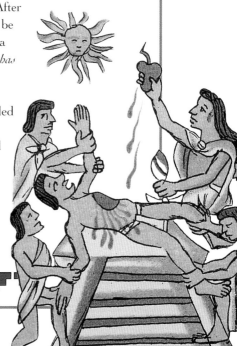

'Dump them in the river?'

'Yes. But grind up the bones first, then sprinkle them on the water.' Which is exactly what they did.

'Well, that's the end of Hunahpu and Xbalanque!' said the triumphant Lords of Xibalba, celebrating.

But it wasn't.

Five days later, down in the shallows of the river, something began to stir. Grains of bonemeal massed together and took form. Catfish – two of them! With their whiskery barbels and streamlined shapes, they slid through the water like snakes.

The next day the catfish were gone, and on the bank stood two men, ragged and tattered. *Chukka-chukk* sang their rattles, *wooh-oo* sang their flutes, as they danced the Dances of the Armadillo, of the Weasel, of the Poorwill, the Dance of the Swallowed Sword. They were wandering performers with a whole bag of tricks. They could walk on stilts. They could perform impossible acts, such as setting a house on fire but not burning it down; such as sacrificing each other but not dying. Soon everyone in Xibalba, just everyone, was talking about them.

One Death and Seven Death wanted to see these paragons for themselves and sent their messengers to fetch them.

'Oh, no,' said the strangers. 'We can't come. Just look at us, in our tatters and rags. How could we go before such great lords looking like this?' And they made a great show of reluctance, but in the end were prevailed upon to go.

They came humbly into the presence of One Death and Seven Death, and prostrated themselves before them.

'Where is your citadel? Your home? Who are your tribe, your mother and father?' the Lords enquired.

'We do not know,' came the reply. 'We are nameless orphans.'

The Lords, eager for the show to begin, did not pursue the matter further and the performance started, to a packed hall.

'Sacrifice my dog!' called one of the Lords. 'Kill him and bring him back to life.'

So the strangers killed the little dog. But only a moment later he was standing up again, wagging his tail and running to his master. Bravo! How the Xibalbans cheered.

'Set my house on fire!' cried One Death, and in an instant the hall was a roaring inferno, yet no one and nothing was burned.

'Kill! Kill!' the shout went up. 'Do a trick sacrifice.' The strangers removed the heart of a Xibalban, and held up the bleeding organ for the Lords to see. A second later their victim was on his feet, laughing. How the company clapped, how they cheered.

'More, more!' shouted the Lords. 'Sacrifice yourselves!'

Spreading himself out on the ground, one of the strangers allowed himself to be dismembered. His heart was removed. His head rolled away outside. And all the while, his companion danced. 'Get up!' he commanded the corpse and – as if awakening from a pleasant sleep – the dead man stood up unscathed. Had the Lords not seen it with their own eyes, they would never have believed it. The hall was in an uproar of applause.

'Me! Me! Kill me!' screamed One Death and Seven Death in hysterical unison.

'Very well, your Lordships,' said the strangers. 'What have you to fear from Death?' And, holding the sacrificial knife, they plunged it into the breasts of the rulers of Xibalba, first one then the other, and gouged out their dripping, pulsating hearts like men scooping dollops of corn mash from a bowl.

But this time, their victims did not stand up. This time, no life-force quickened their inert forms. The Lords of Death were dead, stone dead, and a great silence fell on all assembled there.

'Yes!' said the strangers. 'We have returned – Hunahpu and Xbalanque! You killed our fathers, One Hunahpu and Seven Hunahpu, but you did not kill us. And now here we are, returned to set matters right. No more will the innocent fall victim to your tricks, but only the worthless and wicked. No more will you receive blood in tribute, but incense made of croton sap. No more will you gorge on human flesh, but on creatures of the forest and plain.'

That is how Hunahpu and Xbalanque limited the powers of Xibalba and made life easier for humankind.

Then, as Venus the Morning Star appeared in the east, the brothers went to the grave of Seven Hunahpu. They attempted to reflesh his bones. They replaced his skull on his skeleton, and told the skull to speak: 'Name the parts of your face, and new flesh will clothe your bones.' But the only features the skull could remember were eyes, nose and mouth, for these were the only ones he had, and so a skull he remained.

The brothers laid the bones of Seven Hunahpu to rest, promising that his name would never be forgotten and that his day would always be kept. And so the custom arose of remembering the dead on the day named Hunahpu.

All the time that the brothers had been away in the underworld, Grandmother Xmucane had been waiting. She had watched the stands of corn in the field and had seen them ripen, dry and be harvested. She knew then that her grandsons were dead, burnt in the oven of Xibalba. She had watched the bare earth for signs of renewal and had seen the fresh green shoots pushing their way into the light. She knew now that her grandsons were reborn and happiness swelled her old heart.

Xmucane took the ears stored in the rafters and burned copal – frankincense – before them in thanks. As the smoke curled around them, she named them and made them holy. And so the custom arose of consecrating ears from the new harvest and storing them in the middle of the house, to keep the spirit of the corn alive.

While the Grandmother was making her offering, Hunahpu and Xbalanque left Xibalba. They headed up into the sky. There they became the Sun and his twin, the full Moon. They were joined by the Four Hundred Boys, the Pleiades. And when the Sun and the Moon and the Stars came to live in the sky, they filled all the heavens with glory.

The Volcano, the Mountain and the Five Eggs

• INCA •

Huayallo Carhuincho was an angry god. He belched fire. He spewed lava. He coughed out clouds of smoke that thickened the air. Only one thing sweetened his temper: a meal of infant flesh, tender, succulent and melting. His love of baby meat was so great that he commanded the people to give him one in two of all their children. And because a well-fed god is a sleeping god the people agreed, to keep the peace.

Huayallo Carhuincho, spirit of the volcano, had total power: there was no one to challenge him.

But then one day a challenge came. On top of a mountain called Pariacaca five eggs appeared. The eggs cracked and out flew five falcons. The falcons became five men: they were the five selves of Pariacaca, the five-in-one, the spirit of the mountain.

'Begone!' said the Mountain to the Volcano. 'I am the new ruler here!'

'Begone yourself!'

'I will fight you with water!'

'I will fight you with fire!'

And so a terrible battle began. The Volcano fought water with fire; the Mountain fought fire with water. The whole world shook and shuddered, and the people hid in terror. The belly of Huayallo Carhuincho rumbled with rage. His breath was so hot that it singed the sky. Opening his mouth, he vomited a stream of boiling matter, which slid down his sides towards the lake and the village where the people lived.

Pariacaca's fingertips crackled with lightning. His voice roared like thunder. Straddling the world with his five selves, he sent rain from the five directions – east, west, north, south and centre. The torrent rushed down his sides towards the lake and the village where the people lived. But the lake was not big enough to contain the oncoming flood, so one of the five selves – the one called Llacsa Churapa – ran on ahead and pushed a mountain into its path. The dammed water formed a new lake and the water in the lake and the rain from above put out the fire of Huayallo Carhuincho, who ran away to the lowlands.

Pariacaca wandered his new domain in the guise of a beggar. He came to a village where the people were having a fiesta. Because of his ragged appearance, no one knew who he really was (as if that should have made a difference). No one invited him to join in the merriment – all except for one girl, who showed some kindness and offered him a drink of *chicha*, corn beer. The villagers' inhospitality made Pariacaca angry. Warning the girl of what he intended to do so that she could escape, he drowned the whole village in a flash flood.

Pariacaca then came to another village, where he found a beautiful young woman, crying. 'What is the matter, Choque Suso?' he said, for that was her name.

'The corn is dying for want of water,' she replied.

Pariacaca had loved Choque Suso at first sight, so it was highly fortuitous that what she wanted was what he excelled at – the bringing of water. He proposed a bargain to her. If he brought water to the crops, would she promise to be his in return? Choque Suso agreed.

The mountain god opened up the dam he had made earlier. Then, with the help of the animals of the earth and the birds of the air in a feat of inspired engineering, he released the pent-up water into hundreds of channels, which snaked across the land and carried the life-saving fluid to the parched corn. The crops were saved. Irrigation had been invented.

Pariacaca and Choque Suso went to live on a rocky summit called Yanacaca, at the head of Cocochollo, the watercourse which they had made. 'I love it here so much,' said Choque Suso. 'I never want to leave.' So Pariacaca turned her into a stone and she never did.

MOTHER RAIN AND THE DWARF

• MAYA •

WHERE THE LAND POINTS its nose into the sea, at Uxmal in the peninsula of Yucatan, an old woman once lived. She had neither husband nor children, and her childlessness was a cause of great sorrow to her.

Knowing that eggs contain the miraculous germ of life, she decided one day to try an experiment. Selecting the finest egg she could find, she wrapped it in a soft cloth and placed it in a warm, dark corner of her hut, close to the hearth, to incubate. Every day she carefully removed the wrapping and checked the shell for signs of cracking, but every day, when she came to look, the shell lay unbroken before her, as smooth and pristine as a pearl.

But at last her patience was rewarded. On opening the cloth as usual, what did she see, cushioned in the shards of the broken shell, but the bonniest baby boy with eyes as deep as ink and skin of copper, all gurgles and dimples and smiles? She was overwhelmed with joy. The experiment had worked. She was a mother!

Being old and having no milk herself to feed the baby, the old dame took him instead to a village wetnurse and, over the course of that first year, looked after his every need with the greatest devotion; nothing was too much trouble when it came to the care of her hatchling. In consequence, the child developed at such an astonishing rate that by the time he reached the anniversary of his birth he could walk and talk as well as a grown man, swelling the bony breast of his aged mother with maternal pride.

But then something untoward happened. The egg-child stopped growing. It was as if he had exhausted, in a single burst, his inborn capacity to develop, as if all his energy was spent. His stubby limbs and torso, which would normally have lengthened over time, taking him from the stockiness of infancy to the slenderness of youth, refused to do so, while his outsized head sat uncomfortably on top of his truncated body. Arrested in the proportions of babyhood, the egg-child was – to put it succinctly – a dwarf.

But no matter. Dwarves might be small but they could, as the old woman knew, have extraordinary gifts. Were not many the offspring of the rain gods? And what about the four *bacab* dwarves, who stood holding up the heavens with their eight fat little arms? Without them, the sky would surely come crashing down. There was something else, too. Like aged dames the world over, the old woman was not quite what she seemed; greater powers lurked in her frail frame than you could possibly imagine. She was not so foolish as to have produced and nurtured her hatchling without knowing, in the marrow of her bones, that a great destiny awaited him.

'Trust me,' she whispered to him. 'One day you will be a great lord.'

It was not long before she decided to put her theory to the test. She told her son to go to the king and challenge him to a contest of strength.

'Ai! Ai!' cried the dwarf. 'Do not make me go. I am weak and small.'

'Small is as small does,' replied his mother and sent him on his way.

When the dwarf came before the king and put forward his proposition, the king, much amused to have such a puny adversary, accepted. To test who was the stronger, he said, they must both lift up a particular stone, of prodigious weight.

'Aiee!' wailed the dwarf, running back to his mother. 'That stone is as heavy as me! I cannot lift it. Look at my little arms, my little hands!'

'Little is as little does,' his mother replied. 'Have faith and you will be strong.' And she sent him on his way.

She was right. When the dwarf's turn came to lift the stone, he found that he could raise it without the slightest difficulty, as if it were no more than a pebble on a path.

A murmur of admiration rippled through the assembled crowd, but the king, irritated that the little man had matched him so easily, proposed another test. The dwarf must build a palace higher than any other in the city; if he did not do this, the king would have him killed.

'Ai! Ai!' howled the dwarf, running back to his mother. 'I am going to die, I am going to die! My little legs are not strong enough to carry all that stone!'

'Strong is as strong does,' replied his mother. 'Now be quiet and go to sleep.' And in the morning when they woke they were no longer lying in a hut, but in a palatial pyramid, which soared above the ground like a mountain above a lake and whose peak was so high that it pierced the clouds.

'You see?' the old woman said.

The king was amazed and annoyed to see himself outdone once again, so he set the dwarf a third challenge. He was to collect two bundles of hard wood, with which each would strike the other over the head.

'Aiee!' cried the dwarf, running home to his mother. 'I am not brave enough to do this – the king will crack my skull!'

'Brave is as brave does,' replied his mother. Then she took some cornmeal and made it into a paste with water and rolled the mixture into a round. This she slapped on to a griddle over the fire and cooked it to make a tortilla.

'Here, put this on your head,' she said and sent him on his way.

The dwarf collected the wood, as instructed, and took the two bundles to the palace. Lifting up his bundle, the king brought it down as hard as he could on the dwarf's head, but the blow, cushioned by the tortilla, left the little man quite unharmed.

Now it was the dwarf's turn. Raising his bundle as high as he could – and you must remember the disadvantage of his size – he swung it down with all the strength his short arms could muster on the royal pate. *Crunch! Smash!* The king's skull cracked open like an eggshell and he died on the spot.

Having proved himself to be a man of courage, the dwarf was proclaimed king in the old one's place, just as his mother had predicted.

As for her, she disappeared shortly afterwards, her task being done, and was never seen again. Occasional sightings have been reported, however. In a village not distant from Uxmal, in an underground passage leading from a deep well, an old woman is said to sit who bears more than a passing resemblance to the dwarf's mother. Her seat is by a river and there she lives, a snake coiled by her side, dispensing water from a jar. But the precious liquid is not freely given and its price is high. In return for water to quench the thirsty land, the crone demands human life – infant life – which she feeds to the serpent by her side. What are the people to do but comply?

That, at any rate, is what the rumours claim. Whether they are true or not only those who have seen say, which is neither you nor I.

MISTRESS OF THE RAIN

• INCA •

A MAIDEN WALKS THE broad plain of the sky and in her hands is a pitcher of water. As she walks, she watches. If she sees that the earth is thirsty she up-ends her pitcher and the rain falls. The maiden is the mistress of the rain, a princess of royal blood placed in the sky to do this one task.

But sometimes one of her brothers, up there with her in the clouds, breaks her pitcher. It cracks and splits the sky with rivulets of fire. It shatters and the sound booms through the universe and makes all the world shudder. This is how thunder and lightning are made.

Some people, of a rational and unimaginative turn of mind, maintain that thunder and lightning can be explained in terms of science, that they are no more than meteorological phenomena brought on by such factors as atmospheric pressure, humidity and temperature.

Others, glancing silently up at the sky, know better.

Fierce and loud, the thunder and lightning are the work of men. Gentle and soft, the rain and snow are the work of a woman.

> *Beautiful princess*
> *your brother*
> *has broken*
> *your vase,*
> *and that is why*
> *it thunders, why lightning flashes*
> *and thunderbolts roll.*
> *But you, princess,*
> *mistress of the rain,*
> *you will give us water*
> *and at other times*
> *your hand will scatter hail,*
> *or snow.*
> *Pachacamac,*
> *Creator of the world,*
> *and our god Viracocha*
> *have given you a soul*
> *and a body*
> *for this sole purpose.*

'The Broken Vase', translated from the Quechua

ANCESTORS AND ANIMALS

Two themes link the stories in this chapter: the founding of ancestral lineages and the characters of different animals. 'The Maya Lords and the Sunrise', 'The Birth of the Blue Hummingbird' and 'The First Inca' are all ancestral epics, telling how a particular tribe gained supremacy over its neighbours. Since the narratives are told from the viewpoint of the ruling group, this rise to power is – naturally enough – shown as divinely sanctioned: the group is a god's 'chosen people'. In common with the Hebrew 'chosen people' of the Bible, the Maya, Aztecs and Incas in these tales submit to destiny and undertake some form of migration before settling in their 'promised land'. As always when myth meets history, these stories may encode factual material disguised as mythical fantasy.

'The Maya Lords and the Sunrise', comes from the last part of the Maya creation epic, the *Popul Vuh*, and displays the same dark humour found in other episodes of the work. 'The First Inca' justifies the establishment of the Inca state as divinely predestined. The first Inca family do not settle in the valley of Cuzco accidentally; a sign they are given proves that they have an absolute right to be there.

'The Birth of the Blue Hummingbird' enshrines the pilgrimage of the Aztecs to their 'promised land'. So that they will recognize it their god Huitzilopochtli describes it very precisely. His slaying or expulsion of rival deities is mythological code for the victory of the Aztecs and their gods over the peoples they subjugated along the way. The birth of the Hummingbird, from the head of Coatlicue, recalls the birth of the Greek goddess Athene from the head of Zeus, and is a powerful metaphor for the supremacy of the new god over an earlier cult.

Another motif in this story which evokes other mythologies is the 'immaculate conception' in which Coatlicue is involved. Like Cavillaca (see page 126) and numerous other goddesses the world over – including the Virgin Mary, the Irish Dechtire and the Greek Danaë – Coatlicue is transformed into the archetypal Pregnant Virgin by an absentee god, who reincarnates in his son.

How Pulque was Made

• AZTEC •

Thе wind came sighing through leaves and grass and in the wind was Quetzalcoatl, dreaming dreams and thinking. Humans had all they needed to live: they had animals for meat, and seeds to grow their own crops, and houses to keep out the rain and cold. But were they *happy*? Did they, as they bent over their everyday tasks, feel a surge of joy in their hearts? Did their souls sing? Did they surrender themselves to laughter? How, Quetzalcoatl thought, could he ensure happiness for humankind?

And then he remembered the beautiful Mayahuel.

So he went to wake the goddess, who was sleeping in her grandmother's house in the sky. 'Wake up, and come with me,' he said, 'and together we will make a drink that will bring happiness to humankind.' And Mayahuel woke and descended to Earth with Quetzalcoatl.

Back in the sky trouble was brewing. Mayahuel's grandmother had discovered that she was gone and she was furious. Now this particular crone was no doting, white-haired old lady exuding love and kindness, but one of the dreaded *tzitzimine*, the star demons who set upon the Sun every dawn and dusk, and try to eat him at solar eclipses. When she saw that Mayahuel had run away she went in pursuit of her, and all her fellow demons went with her.

'We will seize her! We will kill her! We will tear her limb from limb!' raged the star-hag.

With their skull-heads clanging and their tongues lolling and their bones clattering and their snake-tails swinging, the *tzitzimine* dived headfirst from the sky, like a rain of spiders from Heaven. And there before them stood a great forked tree – Mayahuel and Quetzalcoatl transformed. In one branch was the goddess; in the other the god.

As the demons advanced, the tree split in half and the two branches came crashing to the ground. But the grandmother was not so easily fooled. She knew which branch was which. Grabbing the one that was Mayahuel, she tore her

apart with her claws and her teeth and shared the pieces out among her companions. Her revenge completed, she returned to the sky with the other *tzitzimime*.

Quetzalcoatl resumed his normal shape. He gazed sadly at the bones of Mayahuel; they were all that was left of the goddess. He gathered them up and quietly buried them. Then he went away.

For a long time the lonely grave of Mayahuel lay still and silent in the heat of the Sun, in the cool of the pattering rain. And then one day a little shoot poked its head out from the soil. Other shoots came up, too, from the same root, and they grew and they grew and they grew until at last a giant plant stood on the place where Mayahuel lay buried. It was taller than a house and had wide, spiny green leaves and flower stems higher than a man.

That plant was the maguey and in its flesh and fibre Mayahuel lived again.

When people discovered the wonderful plant, they invented all kinds of uses for it. Some took its thorns and used them for letting blood to give to the gods. Some ate parts of its stems and flowers, or made rope or cloth from its leaves.

But others did as Quetzalcoatl had wanted. They cut its central stalk and collected the sweet, white sap that flowed out from the heart of the plant – mother's milk, they called it. They left the juice to ferment, to become *aguamiel*, honey water, and then they distilled it to increase its potency further. They called the fermented drink *pulque* or *octli* and the distilled liquor *tequila*.

And so Mayahuel did not die in vain, for from the plant that grew on her grave came the drink which banishes sadness, which makes the soul sing and the heart surge with joy, which releases us in laughter – as Quetzalcoatl had intended all along.

THE RABBIT WHO FELL FROM HEAVEN

• MIXTEC •

WHEN ARMADILLOS KNITTED and macaws glittered with teeth of brightest emerald, when tortoises could fly and bats took to the sky in cloaks of rainbow feathers, Rabbit decided to visit Heaven.

'Look at me!' he complained to the Maker of Life. 'Why have you made me small when I want so much to be bigger?'

'I can make you bigger,' said the Creator, 'but first you must bring me four things. The skins of a jaguar, a monkey, a lizard and a snake.' Rabbit agreed happily to the bargain.

He set off into the forest. He found Jaguar, dozing in the shade of a tree. 'Tch, tch … sleeping the day away!' he said. 'Well, lazybones, you'll soon wake up when the hurricane gets here. Yes, that big old wind will just pick you up and … whoosh … no, I can't bear to imagine it.' All this was a tissue of lies, of course, but then Jaguar was not to know.

'What can I do to escape?' he asked, terrified.

'Well, I may be small but my heart is big. Let me help you – let me tie you to that big tree. Then the wind can't blow you away.'

And so the grateful Jaguar submitted and allowed himself to be tied up by a creature less than a quarter of his size. As soon as he was bound and helpless, Rabbit picked up a stone. He hit Jaguar on the head with it and killed him, and then skilfully removed his skin.

One skin taken, three skins to take.

Rabbit went further into the forest. He saw Monkey, swinging from a branch. He pretended not to notice him. He took out his knife and began hitting himself on the neck with it. *Thwack*! 'Ha, ha, ha!' he trilled. *Slap*! 'Hee, hee, hee,' he giggled. But with each blow he made sure he was using the blunt edge of the blade.

Then he let the knife fall, went off into the undergrowth and waited.

Monkey was fascinated. He, too, wanted to try this magical object which had the power to make you laugh. He scuttled down from his tree. He picked up the knife. He struck himself on the neck with it. And sliced his throat through, from ear to ear.

Rabbit emerged and skilfully removed Monkey's skin.

Two skins taken, two skins to take.

Rabbit went further into the forest. He saw Lizard, warming himself in a bright patch of sunlight and looking bored.

'Fancy a game?' he asked and picked up what looked like a ball. 'Here – catch!' he called and, as Lizard came running towards him, he threw the object – which was really a heavy, round stone – and killed Lizard with a single blow, then he skilfully removed his skin.

Three skins taken, one skin to take.

Rabbit went further into the forest. He came upon Snake, coiled silently by a rock. He crept as close as he could, then curled up and pretended to be sleeping.

Snake spotted him. A fine, fat rabbit – his favourite food! And asleep, too. He felt almost sorry to take advantage, but then he hadn't eaten for a while and he was hungry. He slithered towards Rabbit and was just about to wrap his muscular coils around the little animal and crush him to death when Rabbit woke and, faster than it takes to turn a hair, sank his teeth into Snake's eyes and pierced him through to the marrow. Snake, like all the others, lay dead, and Rabbit skilfully removed his skin.

Four skins taken, no skins to take.

Rabbit climbed to the sky and flung his booty at the feet of the Maker of Life.

'There!' he said. 'I have done what you wanted. Now make me bigger.'

The Creator looked at the pile before him – Jaguar's black-speckled golden pelt, Monkey's brown fur, the richly textured and patterned skins of Lizard and Snake – and he wondered. How was it possible that an animal as small as Rabbit could have achieved all this? And how much more might he achieve if he were bigger? Could he risk making him all-powerful? No, he could not.

And that is why the Maker of Life decided to break his promise.

He approached Rabbit and stroked him on the back. Rabbit glowed with smug satisfaction and waited for his transformation. It was not long in coming.

The Maker of Life picked him up by the ears and swung him around in ever-widening circles, and as Rabbit whirled outwards his ears stretched and grew longer and longer, like two expanding telescopes. Then the Creator quickly released his grip and sent him spinning – through the blue air, past banks of clouds, across mountain tops, over forests – all the way back down to Earth again.

As Rabbit saw the ground looming towards him, he stretched out his front legs to break his fall and stubbed them, which is why they have been short and stumpy ever since. And as for his eyes, they have never lost that startled expression which they had that day, so long, long ago, when he fell all the way from Heaven.

THE BIRD BRIDE

• CAÑARI •

LONG, LONG AGO IT BEGAN to rain. It rained and it rained and it didn't stop until the whole world was drowned – all the trees, all the fields, all the houses, all the animals, all the people. All, that is, except for two brothers.

When the brothers saw the flood rising, they climbed as fast as they could up a mountain called Huaca-ynan and there they clung for dear life, watching as the water crept closer and closer. Just as they were about to give themselves up for dead, a miracle happened. As the torrent rose, so did the mountain, which continued to poke its head above the waters like an island in the middle of the sea.

Safe on their peak, the brothers waited. The rain stopped. The flood receded. The water flowed back into the rivers and streams and into the fissures in the Earth's face. The Sun came out from behind the clouds and lit a new world. The mud dried, the trees put out fresh leaves and young shoots pushed their way through the soil.

The brothers climbed down the mountainside and in the valley below they built a little house for themselves from the wood that was littered about, and roofed it with reeds and leaves. When it was finished, they made a cheerful fire and sat down to contemplate what their new life might bring.

From now on, their days fell into a regular pattern. They woke when the Sun rose and went out to forage for wild herbs and berries and roots and whatever they could find to complement their meagre diet. When the Sun set, they sat by the fire and ate and talked.

Life continued in this uneventful way until one day, as the brothers were returning home, a delicious aroma came wafting towards them on the soft evening breeze. It was an aroma that opened the floodgates of memory, recalling long-forgotten feasts of roast meats, fat and succulent, dripping their juices into a crackling fire; of fragrant herbs which scented the air; of roots and fruits as sweet as honey. Hunger must have deranged their senses, the brothers thought, for such food was not to be had here.

But they were wrong.

On reaching their little house, they were amazed to see a bright fire burning and a meal prepared of all the foods they had imagined, with *chicha* to drink, too. As for the cook, he or she was nowhere to be seen. Who – or indeed what – was their benefactor? But when a man is hungry such questions are only for fools, and the brothers wasted no time in falling upon the meal and eating and drinking until their thirst was slaked and their bellies were full and their chins dripped with the mingled juices of food and *chicha*. And when at last they could eat no more, they fell into a delicious slumber so deep that neither storm nor demon could have disturbed it.

And so it continued the next day and the next until ten full days had gone by, at which point curiosity finally overcame the elder brother and he decided to stay behind when the younger brother went out, to see what he might see.

Well, he waited and he watched – one hour, two hours, three. He had almost dozed off from boredom when he was startled by a swishing sound as two macaws came fluttering down outside the little house. They were the strangest macaws he had ever seen for, although they had wings and feathers like other birds, they were carrying baskets and wore the *llicella*, the mantle, over their hands. And when they removed their mantles and took off their feather cloaks, he saw that they were not birds after all, but beautiful, beautiful women.

'It is you!' he cried, stepping from his hiding place. 'You are the ones who have fed us, who have saved us from starvation! How can we ever thank you?'

Foolish man, to speak so boldly. The bird-women knew that they had been discovered and, according to the laws governing supernatural beings, that would not do. They took one look at the elder brother, gathered up their baskets and their cloaks and flew off, in a flurry of bright feathers. And when the younger brother returned at the end of the day, his welcome was an unlit fire and an empty pot.

It was ten days before the bird-women came again – and a meagre time the brothers had of it – but when on the afternoon of the tenth day they finally arrived, the younger brother was ready.

No sooner had they entered the house, put down their baskets and removed their cloaks, than he covered the doorway. One of the women was too fast for him and escaped through the opening, but the younger one, who moved more slowly, found herself shut in.

She agreed to stay with the brothers and became the wife of the younger, in time bearing three daughters and three sons, who in turn bore children of their own. And so it went on from one generation to another until a whole new tribe had been made.

And that, say the Cañaris of Ecuador, is how they came to be. A macaw was their mother and her sister was the mother of all the macaws in the forest.

THE FIRST INCA

• INCA •

HERE FOLLOWS THE TRUE history of Ayar Manco known as Manco Capac, the first Inca and son of the Sun as the *quipucamayoqs*, the record-keepers, have it.

Long, long ago Con Ticci Viracocha made the first human beings from the clay of the shore of Lake Titicaca. He sent them to wait in the caves and the springs and the mountains. When he called them, they came out, blinking, into the light and settled in their allocated regions.

But, deep in their hiding place in the Earth, a few still waited for his call. They were the lordly ones, Viracocha's chosen people, destined to rule over all the others. They slept in a cave called Capac Toco, the Window of Riches, in a mountain called Tambo Toco, the House of Windows, at a place place called Pacaritambo, the House of Dawn. When they heard the god's voice in their dreams, they rose and came out of the mouth of the cave. They were eight in all, four brothers and four sisters: Ayar Manco and Ayar Auca and Ayar Cachi and Ayar Uchu; Mama Ocllo and Mama Huaco and Mama Cura and Mama Raua.

They were the first of the Inca race.

At the same time, others came out from Maras Toco and Sutic Toco, two caves on either side. They were the first of the Maras and the Tambos.

The lordly ones looked around them. 'We need land – good land,' they said, 'where we can grow our crops and make our home. We will go in search of it, and we will be rulers of the people.' To help them in their conquests, they gathered together ten *ayllus*

or tribes from around the mountain, among them the Maras and Tambos, and promised them territory and riches.

Then the eight brothers and sisters set off, with their followers marching behind. They travelled north-eastward, across mountains which spread over the landscape like folds of crumpled brown paper. In his hand, Ayar Manco carried a golden staff to test the fertility of the soil.

At the first place they stopped – Huanacancha – Ayar Manco pushed his staff into the ground. It met only stones and grit: the soil here was no good. That night, Ayar Manco lay with his sister Mama Ocllo and she conceived a child.

At the second place they stopped – Tambo Quiro – the soil was also poor. Here, Mama Ocllo gave birth to the child she was carrying, a boy. His birth was celebrated with due ceremony and he was given the name Sinchi Roca.

At the third place they stopped – Palluta – the soil was better, so here they settled for a year or two. But in time, the urge to find new and better territory came upon them again, and they moved on.

At the fourth place they stopped – Haysquisro – matters came to a head.

All this time, Ayar Cachi, the third of the brothers, had been causing trouble. Especially strong and fierce, he was a master of the sling and could split mountains with his shot, sending the debris up into the clouds (the ravines which he created may still be seen). But his bellicose nature would not allow him to live peaceably with others: he had shown cruelty to the peoples they had encountered and had fomented disagreements between his brothers and sisters and their followers.

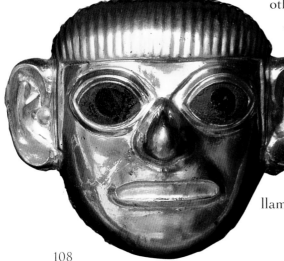

'If this continues,' said Ayar Manco secretly to the others, 'our troops will leave us and we will be alone. We cannot let that happen.' They knew what they had to do: they must get rid of Ayar Cachi.

'Dear brother,' said Ayar Manco to Ayar Cachi, 'how forgetful we have been! Do you remember the cave from which we came? Do you remember the treasures we had there? The *topacusi*, the golden cup? The seeds? The *napa*, the little llama made of gold, which is the emblem of our

nobility? Well – fools that we are – we have left them behind! Return to Capac Toco and fetch the treasures for us.'

'Why me?' replied an irritable Ayar Cachi. 'Why can't someone else go? It's too far. I'm tired. It's late. My feet are sore. My legs ache. My eyes …'

'Be quiet!' interrupted his sister Mama Huaco, stamping her foot in fury and turning all her scorn on him. 'Are you a man or a lazy coward? Do what your brother tells you. Now!'

And so Ayar Cachi was shamed into going. A travelling companion went with him, Tambochacay by name – an assassin, in fact, with secret orders to kill. When the unsuspecting Ayar Cachi entered the cave to retrieve the sacred objects, Tambochacay quickly rolled a boulder over the entrance and walled him up inside. The rage of the imprisoned Ayar Cachi was so great it made the mountain shake. He cursed his jailer for his betrayal and by the power of his magic words transformed him into stone.

Eight brothers and sisters set out from Capac Toco. Now there were only seven.

When they had mourned the sad but necessary death of Ayar Cachi, the survivors moved on.

At the fifth place they stopped – Quirirmanta – a mountain rose before them and they began to climb it. Halfway up its slope they came upon a *huaca*, an object of veneration, shaped like a man. So lifelike was it that it looked exactly like Ayar Uchu, the youngest of the brothers.

His siblings laughed. 'We have here your twin,' they said. 'Go on – see if you can lift him, and we will bring him with us.'

Ayar Uchu climbed on to the statue, which slowly turned its head to look at him. But no matter how hard he pushed and pulled, it refused to move. And when he tried to climb down he found he could not move either. He was bound to the statue by the soles of his feet. A strange and heavy coldness began to seep into his bones.

'Go!' he said to his brothers and sisters. 'Go, and leave me here. Remember me always, and honour me with the first of your offerings. When you celebrate the *huarochicu*, the arming of the warriors, bring the young men to me. I am their father and I will bless them with nobility and valour.'

So saying, Ayar Uchu fell silent, transformed to everlasting stone.

Others say it happened differently – that he flew to heaven in the form of a great bird. They say he talked with Inti the Sun and that, having done so, he returned. Be that as it may, the end was the same: Ayar Uchu was turned to stone on the mountain.

Eight brothers and sisters set out from Capac Toco. Now there were only six.

With grief in their hearts, the survivors continued their ascent of the mountain. When they reached its summit, they saw, spread out below them like a welcoming blanket, a rich and rain-washed valley. Suspended in the sky above it was a rainbow – a *huanacauri* – a most favourable omen. And when Ayar Manco hurled his golden staff down into the valley, it sank the full length of its shaft into the deep and fertile soil.

They had found their homeland at last.

It was here that Ayar Manco changed his name. He became Manco Capac, the Supreme Rich One. He did this, some say, on the instructions of Inti the Sun, relayed to him by Ayar Uchu on his return from heaven.

The mountain on which he stood was given a name, too: it was called Huanacauri in memory of the rainbow. It became the most sacred of hills, and the stone-bound Ayar Uchu, standing on its slope, was venerated before all other *huacas*, being called Ayar Uchu Huanacauri.

The survivors descended the mountain, down into the fertile valley.

At the sixth place they stopped – Matahua – they decided to stay awhile. It was here that Sinchi Roca, the son of Manco Capac, became a man. He was given arms and his ears were pierced as a sign of his nobility and warriorhood, in accordance with the rites of the *huarochicu* when youths pass into manhood. His father and his mother and his uncle and his aunts all celebrated his coming of age. Dressed in purple robes, they danced the royal dance called *capac raymi*, which would be danced again by many generations to come, at the *ayuscay*, when a baby is born; at the *rutuchico*, when an infant's hair is first cut; and at the *quicochicuy*, when a girl comes of age.

It was at Matahua, too, that they first sang the song for the dead, a sad and soft ululation which sounded like the cooing of doves.

They spent two years at Matahua and then they moved on, into the upper part of the valley.

At the seventh place they stopped – Huanaypata – Manco Capac looked a little way ahead, near the spot where his golden staff had sunk into the soil. Beckoning to Ayar Auca, he said, 'Brother, do you see that pile of stones, a short distance from where we stand? That is where we will build our city, where we will establish our rule. Go, and take possession of it.'

And Ayar Auca obeyed. Turning himself into a great bird, he flew off and alighted on the heap of stones, where he became the stone that marked the Inca claim to the site.

Eight brothers and sisters set out from Capac Toco. Now there were only five.

So it was that at Huanaypata, six leagues from where they had started, Manco Capac and his sisters founded their city. They called it Cuzco, which means 'navel', for it was the centre of all life.

Laid out in the shape of a puma, a sacred animal of power, with a fortress as its head and a river as its spine, Cuzco grew to be the wonder of the world. In time, it swelled to accommodate a population of 15,000, who walked its paved streets, lived in its stone houses, worshipped in its temples of gold and silver, benefited from its advanced water supply system, and knew no poverty.

In Cuzco, Manco Capac became the first king: he was the Inca, the son of the Sun. When his reign ended, he was succeeded by his own son Sinchi Roca and so a dynasty was founded and the seeds of an empire were sown, which stretched north, south, east and west, across Peru, into Chile and Argentina, into Ecuador. The empire was called Tahuantinsuyu, which means the Four United Quarters, and its like has never been seen before or since.

Such is the true history of Ayar Manco known as Manco Capac, the first Inca and son of the Sun, as the *quipucamayoqs* have it.

FRUITS OF THE EARTH

Two of the world's most popular foods – potatoes and chocolate – are of South and Central American origin.

Potatoes were a staple food of the Inca empire, and were grown in the valleys of the Andes. Hundreds of varieties were developed from the original wild tuber; frost-resistant *chuno* potatoes were, and are, a favourite in the highlands. *Chuno* is also the name of a type of potato flour used to make bread. The potato was introduced to Spain and England in the mid-1500s.

Although it is not a staple food, chocolate is one substance that many people cannot do without. It is made from the seeds of the cacao tree ('cocoa' being a corruption of 'cacao'), and was one of the most important crops in Mesoamerica. The Maya of the Classic period, beginning in 200 CE, were familiar with it, and vases dating from this time are now known to have been chocolate drinking vessels. A favourite of rich Mesoamericans, the frothy drink was made by grinding the beans to powder, and then mixing it with water and flavourings.

Cacao beans were also used as currency; the Maya of Yucatán were still trading with them as late as the nineteenth century. The *conquistador* Hernándo Cortés took cacao beans back to Spain in 1528.

One of the oldest food plants of Central America is maize, or corn; the earliest known cultivated maize can be dated back to 3500 BCE in southern Mexico. It was the principal ingredient of the Maya and Aztec diets, and was prepared in various ways – some of which will be familiar to those who enjoy Mexican cuisine today. The Maya made flat cornmeal pancakes which we know by their Spanish name: tortillas. They also made an alcoholic drink from corn called *balche*, to which they added honey and spice. Among the Aztecs, the cornmeal pancake was known as the *tlaxcalli* and was used to scoop up other foods, or wrapped around meat or vegetables to make *tacos*.

The cultivation of maize spread south and became important to the Incas, who used it in cooking and to make *chicha*, corn beer. In imperial times, brewing *chicha* was a task reserved for the 'chosen women' of the Inca court; today it is poured on the earth as a libation during sowing and harvesting ceremonies in the Peruvian highlands.

Chilli peppers, beans, avocadoes, squash and sweet potatoes were also cultivated. The Incas grew an edible root called *oca*, and both the Incas and Aztecs valued certain grains belonging to the amaranth genus. These were used both as everyday foods and as ritual food in religious ceremonies – which is why their cultivation was banned by the Vatican.

Tomatoes, which were native to South America, were another new vegetable found in Mexico by the Spanish, who introduced them into Spain in the mid-1500s.

THE MAYA LORDS AND THE SUNRISE

• MAYA •

IN THE TIME BEFORE THE dawn, the gods made humankind. It was Sovereign Plumed Serpent and Hurricane, Heart of Heaven, who did this, moulding men and women from the cornmeal ground on her grinding stone by Grandmother Xmucane.

The gods gave names to the first four men. They called them Jaguar Quitze, Jaguar Night, Not Now and Dark Jaguar. To bring them happiness, they gave them beautiful wives. They called the wives Red Sea Turtle, Prawn House, Water Hummingbird and Macaw House.

The brothers and their wives had children and so began the great lineages of the Quiché Maya. And the other humans whom the gods made also multiplied, so that soon there was a great throng of peoples: black ones and white ones, tribes of the mountains and the grasslands, tribes who spoke in different tongues. Starting from the east they spread out, watching the sky as they wearily wandered the world, waiting for the Morning Star to call the Sun into being, waiting for the light to come.

Jaguar Quitze and Jaguar Night and Not Now and Dark Jaguar set off with their wives for the citadel Tulan Zuyua, the place of the Seven Caves and Seven Canyons. It lay in the mountains to the east and they hoped to make it their home.

When the brothers reached the city, each received his own patron god and became a great lord. Jaguar Quitze had one-legged Tohil. Jaguar Night had Auilix; Not Now had Hacauitz. Dark Jaguar had his own god, too: he was called Middle of the Plain.

But the Quiché Maya and their Lords were not the only ones in the city. Members of other tribes had gathered there as well and now it was full. In the dark sunless air, it was also cold, very cold. As the people huddled around their fires, it began to rain and the rain turned to hail and the hailstorm put out the flames, which were their only source of warmth. How their teeth chattered and their bones shivered!

But the Lords were lucky for they had Tohil on their side. Standing with his one leg placed firmly in his sandal, the god went into a spin. He turned faster and faster until his leg became a shaft of lightning sending out sparks in all directions and kindling a new fire in the ashes of the old.

All the people crowded round. 'Give us fire!' they cried. 'We are so cold.'

'Tell them', Tohil said, 'that they may have fire if they agree to embrace me, if they agree one day to be suckled by me.'

'We agree,' the people replied. They did not realize that Tohil spoke in the language of riddles; that his words did not mean what they thought. Later they would discover, to their cost, the true meaning of the promise they had made. But for now they were content just to be warm.

Tohil then spoke again to the Quiché Lords. 'Tulan Zuyua is not for you. Come, it is time to be on the road again, to look for your true home.'

Jaguar Quitze and his brothers bled their ears and elbows in homage, then they and their wives left the city, gazing back at it as they went and singing a song of farewell, for their hearts were heavy with sadness. They carried their gods on their backs.

As they journeyed south-west, certain other tribes, who had been with them in the city, went too. On the way they passed the ancient ballcourt where the sons and grandsons of Xmucane – One Hunahpu and Seven Hunahpu, Hunahpu and Xbalanque – once played ball.

At last they reached a great mountain, so they gathered together to take counsel and to give the tribes their names. From that day on, the mountain where the people had met and named the names was called the Place of Advice.

Up on the mountaintop the Lords and their wives fasted, and all the time they were watching the sky, waiting for the Morning Star to call the Sun into being, waiting for the light to come.

Here Tohil spoke to them again, and Auilix and Hacauitz.

'It is nearly time for the dawn,' the gods said. 'Hide us in secret places so that no one can steal us away, so that we can be your gods for ever.' So the Lords carried them off into the forest of pines and bromeliads and mosses. They placed Auilix in a canyon, Hacauitz on a mountaintop and Tohil on another peak. And the places where the gods hid took their names.

Up on the mountain called Hacauitz, the Lords of the Quiché Maya waited for the sunrise. When at last the Morning Star appeared, their hearts filled with happiness, for this was a sign of what would soon come. They unwrapped the copal incense they had brought with them and burned it in gratitude, and its scent and its smoke floated up into the lightening sky. And as they watched, the sky grew brighter and reddened and the Sun, in all his fiery splendour, rose for the first time above the eastern horizon.

He shone on all the people, who stood waiting for his arrival, on Hacauitz and in places near and far. And although the people were apart, they were as one under the same sunrise. They rejoiced and all creation rejoiced with them. The parrot squawked; the eagle and the vulture performed aerobatics in the air; the puma and the jaguar purred their deep-throated purrs.

In the wake of the Sun came the Moon and the Stars. But the Sun was very hot. His face glared, his body blazed, and in the burning glance of his eye he dried up the muddy face of the Earth and turned gods and animals to stone. Tohil, Auilix, Hacauitz and all the wild beasts of the forest were petrified where they stood. Only one escaped this fate by hiding in the shade of the trees. He was a small, insignificant god called White Sparkstriker, and he became the guardian of the stone animals. In forests and caves he may still be seen, and on dark nights and in dreams. He dresses all in red, the colour of the dawn.

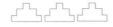

After the first sunrise, the Quiché Lords settled at Hacauitz and built their citadel there. But they and their people were few in number compared with the other tribes, whom they saw from their mountain fastness thronging the roads of the world.

The life the Quichés lived out there in the forest was a simple one. Their food was the larvae of yellowjackets, wasps and bees. When they went to sacrifice before their stone gods they brought the humblest of offerings. They gave blood drawn from their ears and elbows, they burned resin from trees and pieces of bark and marigolds.

And when the gods drank the blood and received the offerings, they were refreshed and stepped out of the heart of the rock in the form of youthful spirits and walked and talked with the Quiché Lords.

'We are hungry,' said Tohil. 'Bring us the blood of the deer and the birds.' So Jaguar Quitze and Jaguar Night and Not Now and Dark Jaguar went out hunting in the forest and gave the gods animal blood to drink and bundles of deerskin.

But such a diet was not enough to sustain a god, not enough to ensure his favour, to show him gratitude, and the Lords began to look elsewhere for their offerings, at the members of other tribes. They watched them from their hiding places in the forest, as they walked by in ones and twos along the roads of the world. They called out in the voices of animals – of the fox, the coyote, the puma and jaguar – so that the travellers would not know they were there and would think that only beasts inhabited the forest.

It was then that Tohil reminded them of an old promise. 'Do you remember Tulan Zuyua?' he said. 'Do you remember how I gave fire to the tribes if they promised to let me suckle them? I wish to suckle them now.'

The Lords remembered and understood.

Now they began to do more than merely watch the lonely travellers: they began to seize them. They dragged them before Tohil, Auilix and Hacauitz, cut them open and let the gods drink their blood. That is how the gods gave suck.

When the Lords had done with them, they rolled their victims' skulls out on the roads. When the other tribes found them, they thought that the killings were the work of wild beasts. But then they began to suspect the Quichés and their gods.

The tribes came together for a great meeting. 'We are many and they are few,' they said. 'We can defeat them.' And they set off to search for the killers of their people. They searched for them despite mud and mist, despite cloud and storm, but all they found were the footprints of the jaguar, the footprints of the deer. And then they discovered the river where the gods, as spirit youths, came to bathe; it was called Tohil's Bath. Tohil and Auilix and Hacaulitz were seen there many times, but would vanish as soon as they were sighted.

How could the tribes defeat these gods? How could they get the better of them? The solution became clear. The gods were youths: they would be tempted by maidens. So two beautiful girls were chosen from among the tribes. Their names were Lust Woman and Wailing Woman. They were told to go to the riverbank on the pretext of washing their clothes.

'If the gods make advances to you, you must yield,' said their elders, 'but ask them for gifts, and these will be proof that you have spoken with them.'

Lust Woman and Wailing Woman set off for the river, dressed in all their finery. When they reached the bank, they removed all their clothes so that they were naked. Then they knelt down on the rocks and began to do their washing. That is how Tohil, Auilix and Hacauitz first encountered them when they came to the river to bathe. But they were not in the least tempted.

'Who are you and what do you want here?' they demanded. And when the maidens explained that they had been sent to speak with them, and to bring back some small gifts as a sign, the gods went away to the Quiché Lords and told them what to do. And this is what they did: they made three exquisite cloaks. Into the weave of the first a jaguar was worked, the emblem of Jaguar Quitze. Into the weave of the second, an eagle, the emblem of Jaguar Night. And into the third, the emblems of Not Now – swarms of yellowjackets and wasps which were so lifelike that you could almost hear them buzz.

The Lords themselves delivered the gifts to the maidens. 'Take these to your masters,' they said, 'and tell them to put them on.'

Lust Woman and Wailing Woman returned to their people and gave them the presents they had brought. The first lord put on the jaguar cloak. It was magnificent. He twirled around in it and paraded himself before all those present. The second lord put on the eagle cloak. It was even finer than the first: he could almost imagine himself flying. The third lord put on the cloak of yellowjackets and wasps … and the insects rose in a great swarm from the cloth and stung him in every part of his body.

In disgrace for bringing such humiliation, Lust Woman and Wailing Woman were spurned. Having been given the role of temptresses, that is what they remained: they became the first prostitutes.

The tribes met once again. 'We are many and they are few,' they said and they armed themselves for battle. They were a mighty army, more than twenty-four thousand strong, bristling with spears and lances and axes. They set off to seize the citadel of Hacauitz and to take the Quiché gods as their prize. They went by night, believing that the cover of darkness would be to their advantage.

But on the road they were overcome by a deep and enchanted sleep, and while they slumbered, the Quichés came down from their fortress and plucked out their eyebrows and shaved off their beards and stripped their headdresses and cloaks and staffs of their metal trimmings, so that when their enemies awoke in the morning and felt their faces they were as naked as a newborn babe's.

Angered by such humiliation, the tribes continued towards Hacauitz.

'We are many and they are few,' they said.

And so it turned out to be, for when their scouts went ahead to reconnoitre, they saw only a small number of warriors stationed behind the wooden palisade surrounding the citadel; they were wearing the metal ornaments which they had taken during the night.

'Victory is ours!' the scouts reported back to their masters.

And the vast army prepared to attack with a great deal of sound and fury.

Inside the palisade Jaguar Quitze and Jaguar Night and Not Now and Dark Jaguar stood, with their wives and families. They watched as their enemies advanced, howling and bellowing and crying their battle cries. But they were not afraid – which is surprising given their small number, and given that the warriors behind the palisade were no more than wooden mannikins, put there for show.

The truth is that they had a secret weapon, which Tohil had told them to make and they were ready to use it when the moment was right.

That moment had come.

Just as their enemies were about to breach the fence, they opened the four gourds they had placed at its corners. And out flew the angry creatures imprisoned inside them – wasps and yellowjackets in their thousands. The buzzing swarm fell upon the invaders.

They stung them on their eyelids.

They stung them on their lips.

They stung them in their ears.

They stung them on all the soft and tender parts of their bodies.

The warriors panicked. They turned and ran, bumping into each other and stumbling in their frenzy to escape. Still the black, buzzing cloud pursued them. And when the Quichés and their women set about them with ordinary weapons, they were as easy to defeat as frightened children.

'As long as there is day, as long as there is light, you shall pay us tribute,' the Lords told them.

And so it was. From that moment on, all the tribes were subservient to the Quiché Mayas, who multiplied and prospered on Hacauitz mountain.

Surrounded by their families, Jaguar Quitze and Jaguar Night and Not Now and Dark Jaguar grew old. They knew that death was near.

'A new year is coming,' they said, 'and the Lord Deer will rule it from his home in the east. It is to the east we must go, back to where we came from.'

Then Jaguar Quitze gave to his kin a sacred, cloth-swaddled bundle which must never, he said, be unwrapped. It was called the Bundle of Flames.

'Keep this in memory of me. And when you wish to ask things of me, burn offerings before it,' he told them.

And so saying, he and his three brothers raised their voices in a song of farewell – the same song they had sung when leaving Tulan Zuyua. And then they were gone, back to their tribal home in the east.

They were never seen again.

A SACRED LANDSCAPE

The Incas and their subjects inhabited a sacred landscape whose geological features were suffused with the numinous. The holy sites and objects which filled this landscape were known as *huacas*. Caves, mountain peaks, springs, boulders or pillars of stone could all be *huacas* and the beliefs surrounding them reflected an intimate bond with the Earth out of which, in myth, human beings had come.

In the creation story in which Viracocha makes the first humans from clay, he returns them to their various caves, springs and mountains to await the call to life. When they hear the call and rise up, they are, figuratively, born out of the soil on which they stand and their tribal places of 'birth' – whatever they may be geologically – are sacred. Such a concept reflects the orderly Inca world view – a place for every people, and every people in their place – which rooted each tribe or *ayllu* (kinship group) in the region where they lived.

Caves were often venerated as tribal places of origin. The place where an *ayllu* had originated at 'birth' was the place to which its members returned in death. In the seventeenth century, when the Spanish were trying to root out 'idolatrous' native practices, they discovered caches of mummies in caves in the central highlands of Peru which ranged in number from 214 to 728. These mummified ancestors were worshipped, given fresh clothing at particular times of the year, and presented with offerings of food at planting and harvest.

Stones, boulders and mountain peaks all had their own indwelling spirits who were personifications of these geological forms. In the origin myth of the Inca state, the three brothers of Manco Capac – Ayar Cachi, Ayar Uchu and Ayar Auca – are respectively entombed in their cave of origin or turned to stone along the way, and thus become *huacas* marking the legendary progress of the first Inca family from their cavernous birthplace to the site of Cuzco, capital of the Inca empire.

Being encased in stone did not necessarily signify immobility and there were myths about mountain peaks which could move. Pariacaca, a high summit and *huaca* in his personified form was able to roam the countryside as a hero or local god in the province of Huarochirí in Peru's central highlands.

Mountain peaks were some of the most powerful *huacas*, but large or notable boulders might be sacred, too. These were called *huancas* and contained the spirits of the ancestors of the local people.

Although such beliefs may seem primitive, there is a similar tradition in Western mytho-religion, which says that mud and rock are the flesh and bones of the Earth, from which we have come and to which we return.

THE LLAMA WHO WOULD NOT EAT

• INCA •

IN THE DAYS WHEN ANIMALS could speak and humans could understand what they said, there lived a man who owned a llama. Theirs was a mutually helpful relationship: the man made sure that the llama had enough to eat and protected him from the pumas which roamed the mountains; the llama, in return, served the man as a beast of burden and provided him with wool for his clothing. This two-way arrangement suited them both admirably.

What, then, was the man's surprise when, on leading the llama to a patch of the finest pasture one day, the animal refused to be tethered to graze. Indeed, he would not so much as sniff at the succulent grass beneath his nose and showed signs of the greatest grief and torment, inasmuch as any animal can.

The llama's apparent obstinacy exasperated the man beyond endurance. 'Ingrate!' he shouted. 'Do I not find for you the best pasture in all the mountains? Do I not care for you as if you were my own flesh and blood? And what thanks do I get? You refuse to eat! Do you not know that without food your body will wither and your wool will fall, and what good will you be to me then?'

'Idiot!' retorted the llama. 'If you had taken the trouble to question me as to why I cannot eat, you would have gained a little understanding. Do you not know that in five days from now the sea will cover the whole world and drown all the creatures in its path?'

The master was aghast at the llama's words and felt greatly humbled.

'Is there no way to escape?' he asked. 'I do not want to die.'

'There is one way,' the llama replied. 'You must collect enough food for five days and follow me to the top of the mountain called Villca-Coto. There we will wait for the flood.'

So the man did as the llama had instructed. He collected potatoes, corn and hot peppers, and water for drinking, and when all was ready and loaded on the llama's back, master and beast set off for the mountaintop.

The climb to the summit was long and steep, for Villca-Coto was higher than all the other mountains. When they finally reached the peak, the man was surprised to see that they were not alone, for all the animals and birds in the world were already gathered there.

There were the vicuña and the guanaco, the llama's wild cousins. There were the pampas cat, the Andean cat and the deer of the highland forest. There were the guinea-pig, the hog-nosed skunk and the mountain viscacha. There were the land predators – the puma, fox, and weasel – all resisting the temptation to eat their fellows in deference to the seriousness of the occasion.

And perched on every rocky ledge, on every outcrop, were birds, numberless birds – the red-backed and puna hawks, the harrier, eagle and falcon, the singing sierra-finch, miner and seedsnipe, the mountain-tanager, flycatcher, furnarid and hummingbird – and above them all, floating on the updraughts of air like a dream in the mind of God, was the giant condor.

The man settled down as best he might amidst the throng and waited to see what would happen. From his vantage point on the mountaintop, all the world was in view, from sierra and rainforest to pampas and plain. And as he gazed westward, the sea slowly began to rise, just as the llama had predicted. It crept across the shore. It stretched out its fingers to caress the foothills. It swelled to rise up the slopes. It opened its mouth to swallow the lower peaks. And as the fifth day came all the mountains except for Villca-Coto had disappeared beneath the water. Now the flood was even licking its way up that great peak, forcing the creatures who had taken refuge there to crowd further together. In the scramble for space, the fox let the end of his tail fall into the water. From that day on, the tip of the fox's tail has been black.

As the day came to a close, the rising tide finally slackened, the sea began to recede, and all the creatures were able to make their way down the mountain.

Of the human race, none but the llama's master had survived. It is as well that he heeded his animal's words. Had he not, I would not be here to tell this tale and you would not be here to know it, for it is from him that all the people on Earth are descended.

A llama wished
to have golden hair,
brilliant as the sun,
strong as love
and soft as the mist
that the dawn dissolves,
to weave a braid
on which to mark,
knot by knot,
the moons that pass,
the flowers that die.

From *Memory of Fire*, Eduardo Galeano

CONIRAYA AND THE ANIMALS

• INCA •

CONIRAYA VIRACOCHA HAD the power of creation at the tip of his tongue. He had only to say 'Be!', and it was. He called the fields into being and the terraces that climbed the mountainsides. He made the irrigation canals which carried water to the thirsty earth by throwing down a flowering *pupuna* reed; the flower's segments became the water channels. He made the villages in which the people lived.

Now you would think that a god of such greatness would be a magnificent being, radiating divine glory. But you would be wrong. For reasons best known to himself, Coniraya disguised himself as a beggar, and in rags he wandered the world. Seeing only the outer man and not the inner god, people would push him off their doorsteps and chase him down the street: 'Be off with you, you filthy tramp! On your way, you miserable wretch! We don't want your kind here.' Ducking their blows, Coniraya would take to the road once more.

But one day Coniraya saw a sight that stopped him in his tracks: a young woman of the most ravishing beauty. Her hair was long and black and as sleek as a cat's. Her skin was smooth and honey-coloured. Her eyes were dark pools which sparkled like the stars in the indigo night. Her movements had the grace of a puma. Her name was Cavillaca and Coniraya wanted her more than he had ever wanted anything.

'Good-day to you, my pretty one. May I walk a little way with you?' he asked.

Cavillaca looked him up and down. 'You? Walk with me? Never!' she said. And tossing her mane of hair, she turned on her heel and ran off.

It is a cruel trick of nature's that when the object of our desire is denied us, its power becomes even greater, drawing us helplessly like a magnet. So it was with Coniraya. His rejection by Cavillaca only served to heighten his passion, to make him more determined than ever to satisfy his yearning for her in whatever way he could, be it fair or foul.

He waited for his opportunity. It came at last when Cavillaca was sitting at her loom, in the shade of a *lúcuma* tree, weaving a poncho with many-coloured stripes and patterns. Changing himself into a bird, Coniraya flew up into the tree and settled in its branches, which were laden with fruit. He pierced one with his beak and injected his seed into its sweet, juicy, yellow flesh. Then he loosened it from its stalk. *Plop*! It dropped straight into the lap of the unsuspecting Cavillaca, who picked it up and ate it. Nine months later she found herself giving birth to a baby boy. The event surprised her greatly for, to the best of her recollection, and according to the normal biological standards by which such matters are measured, she was still a virgin.

She was determined to discover the identity of the man who, by devious or magical means, had contrived to make her a mother. So she called all the *vilcas*, the male gods, all the *huacas* – the genii of place – to a meeting. They came in droves, all eager to win her love for, you must understand, she was still a very beautiful woman and highly desirable.

There they all sat, the gods, in their gold and feather finery, casting jealous glances at one another to see who was the handsomest, the most manly. But when Cavillaca put the question, 'Who is the father of my child?', not one of them spoke. So she placed her son, who was toddling by now, on the ground: let him be the judge. With his child's unclouded wisdom, he would know his own father.

Pattering along on his short, plump legs, the little boy bypassed one great lord after another until at last he came to a scruffy-looking individual at the far end of the line. Well, thought Cavillaca, would you believe it? It was the odious tramp whose advances she had so firmly rejected barely more than nine months earlier! What business had he here? The effrontery of it, to come before her now.

The little boy did not share his mother's reservations. Unerringly, he stopped in front of the tramp, clambered into his lap and smiled a dimpled smile of happy recognition. 'Dada!' he said.

Cavillaca was outraged. It simply was not possible that such a loathsome, repellent, hideous, shabby, unsavoury, unclean and – yes – malodorous creature could be the father of her beloved baby. Well, even if he was, she would not accept him. Never, ever! So she picked up her son and, with a flick of her midnight hair, turned on her heel and set off towards the sea.

Naturally, Coniraya followed her, but as she had had a good start he soon lost sight of her. Still, he continued to search for her, the woman he loved, and whenever an animal or bird passed by he would ask it a question. It was always the same: 'Have you seen Cavillaca?'

'Have you seen Cavillaca?' he said to the condor, coasting in his dream on the updraughts of air.

'Yes, I saw her but a moment ago, from my place in the clouds. If you're quick, you'll catch her.'

'A blessing on you,' said Coniraya. 'Your life will be long and your food plentiful, for yours is the carrion of the mountains. Whoever dares to kill you will die.'

'Have you seen Cavillaca?' he said to the skunk, rootling about in the undergrowth.

'Cavillaca? Yes – she walked by when I was digging in the bushes. But that was hours ago. You'll never catch up with her now. If I were you, I'd give up and go home.'

'A curse on you,' said Coniraya. 'Because of your foul odour you will be shunned by humankind. You will hide yourself in shame by day and only come out at night.'

'Have you seen Cavillaca?' he said to the puma, slinking across the path on his soft cat's paws.

'Yes, it is not long since I saw her, from my hiding place in the rocks. If you run, you should catch her.'

'A blessing on you,' said Coniraya. 'Yours will be the power to punish wrongdoers. When you die, men will wear your skin in honour of your greatness.'

'Have you seen Cavillaca?' he said to the fox, sniffing about in the forest.

'Yes, I saw her, from my hole in the earth, but I really couldn't say when. If you're looking for her, I shouldn't bother. She could be anywhere by now.'

'A curse on you,' said Coniraya. 'You will be hated by mankind, who will kill you and all your kind wherever they find you.'

'Have you seen Cavillaca?' he said to the falcon, swooping down from the sky.

'Yes, I saw her when I was hovering over the treetops, not far from here. Run – go on, run after her!'

'A blessing on you,' said Coniraya. 'You will be great among birds, and in death men will honour you.'

'Have you seen Cavillaca?' he said to the parrot, sitting in the branches.

'A woman with a child did go by, when I was flying through the jungle. Now let me see – was it today? No, I tell a lie – it must have been yesterday. Yesterday, today – who cares? She'll be a long way away by now. Be a sensible fellow. Take my advice: go home.'

'A curse on you,' said Coniraya. 'You will chatter ceaselessly in a loud and foolish voice and your screeches will lead your enemies to you.'

At last Coniraya arrived by the seashore at the shrine of Pachacamac. Cavillaca and her son were nowhere to be seen. But Coniraya did spot something else. Two beautiful girls sitting by the water's edge, grooming their hair. They were the daughters of Pachacamac, god of the shrine, and the goddess Urpay Huachac. Apart from the snake who chaperoned them, they were totally – deliciously – alone. How could Coniraya resist?

He sidled up to the elder of the two and, with sweet words and whispered flatterings, 'You are the most beautiful girl I have ever seen … your eyes put the stars to shame … your lips are two ripe fruits, asking to be kissed' – and so on and so forth, he seduced her. But when he tried the same technique on the younger sister – 'Your hair is a cascade of flowers … your teeth a row of shells' – the girl promptly changed herself into a dove and flew away.

Coniraya was furious. He wanted revenge. But how? Then he saw it: the pool in which the girls' mother, Urpay Huachac, kept all her fish. Gathering up armfuls of the wriggling mass, he threw them into the ocean, which is why, to this day, there are fish in the sea. He continued to look for Cavillaca and her son, up and down the coast, but he never found them. If only he had looked a little harder, if only he had attuned his eyes to a different vision, he would have seen them. They stand at the shrine of Pachacamac on the coast of Peru, a short way out to sea. Two rocks, one medium-sized and one small. It is rumoured by the people thereabouts that when the sun hits the water at a certain angle the rocks take on an almost human shape. Some even claim to have seen them move; they claim to have seen the larger of the two reach out, as it were, to the smaller, like a mother taking her child's hand. But perhaps it was just a trick of the light.

Two rocks washed by the ocean: wild birds wheel above them, waves nibble at their feet, fish tickle their toes. In their stony hearts, they guard the memory of an ancient tale.

THE BIRTH OF THE BLUE HUMMINGBIRD

• AZTEC •

WHO HAS SEEN HIM, the blue Hummingbird of the South, waving plumes upon his head, stripes upon his face, the fire-serpent in his hand? Of all the gods he is the greatest: Huitzilopochtli is his name.

Huitzilopochtli whispered to his people the Aztecs, on their lake-isle of Aztlan, the White Place, the Place of Herons, telling them secrets of the future.

'Far away, there is an island in a lake. On the island a cactus grows and on the cactus an eagle sits. There, where the eagle rests, is your new home. Seek it and I will be with you. Seek it and you shall prosper and be the mightiest of races.'

Obeying the great word of Huitzilopochtli, the seven tribes packed up their belongings and set off southwards to the promised land, following their god.

Over hills and valleys they went, over rough ground and smooth, until at last at Chicomoztoc, the Mountain of the Seven Caves whose mouths gave birth to mankind, they stopped. No eagle did they see, no cactus, island or lake. This was not their new home, but here they settled awhile, for the span of a lifetime or two.

It was at Chicomoztoc that divisions split the tribes. Some

began to worship Malinalxochitl, the Hummingbird's sister. Others, remaining true to Huitzilopochtli, decided to go their own way and resumed their nomadic journey, following their god.

Through deserts they went and by the feet of volcanoes. The road was long and hard, but at length, dusty and exhausted, they arrived at Coatepec, Serpent Mountain, home of the goddess Coatlicue, the Lady of the Serpent Skirt.

Coatepec was no more promising than their last stopping place – no eagle sat on a cactus here, on an island in the middle of a lake. But it would do for now and so they made it their home.

How must they have looked, this ragtaggle horde, Huitzilopochtli's chosen people, battered, dirt-caked and weary? How did their dusty encampment compare with glorious Tula, which lay so close by?

Tula, the fabled city, was home to the Toltecs, a noble race famed far and wide for their wealth, the luxuriousness of their lives, the skills of their craftsmen, the achievements of their artists, the wisdom of their healers, the proficiency of their scribes. Huitzilopochtli did not rule here, but other gods, chief among them Quetzalcoatl, the Plumed Serpent. A cultured god of a cultured people, Quetzalcoatl lived in a palace more lavish than fancy can conjure. Indeed, it was not one palace but four, oriented to the four corners of the Earth and adorned with gold, with jade and turquoise, with shells and silver and precious stones.

Huitzilopochtli observed all this and bided his time.

Within the mount of Coatepec, near which the Aztecs were encamped, its custodian Coatlicue was sweeping out her house. As she worked, moving steadily on her taloned feet, her rattlesnake skirt writhing and her necklace of human hearts and hands swinging back and forth over her pendulous breasts, she came upon a ball of feathers, jewel-bright and iridescent as the rainbow. Where could such a treasure have come from? Coatlicue did not know, nor much care, but as she did not want to lose her precious find she tucked the feathers safely away in her clothing, close to her skin. But later, when she looked for them again, they had gone.

A month or so after this Coatlicue experienced a miracle: she had, somehow, participated in an immaculate conception, for she was now carrying a child.

'Who is he? Tell me – who is the father?' raged her daughter Coyolxauhqui on discovering her mother's predicament. 'You have five hundred children already – isn't that enough? Oh, the disgrace of it!'

And the luminous, lunar Lady Golden Bells, nose pendant a-glinting, cheek bells a-flashing, stormed off to spread the bad news amongst her tribe of brothers, the Centzon Huitznahua, the Four Hundred Southerners.

'Kill her! That's what you must do – destroy her! We cannot let her humiliate us in this way!' she screeched.

Fired to battle fury by their sister's vengefulness, the Four Hundred Southerners made ready their weapons and plotted. But Coatlicue remained calm for, from deep within her womb, a still, small voice comforted her.

'Fear not,' it said. 'The child that you bring forth shall be called great among the nations and you, the mother of God, shall for ever be remembered.' And Coatlicue, the unwitting vessel of the coming incarnation, prepared herself for death and everlasting glory.

It was not long in coming. At Coatepec her four hundred sons, wielding lances, axes and blade-studded clubs, chased their mother up the mountain and there at the peak, with their sister urging them on, they sliced off her head. A fountain of blood gushed from the mutilated neck of the Lady of the Serpent Skirt, and on its crest rode the child she had been carrying, conceived through impregnation by a ball of feathers, born in blood and murder – it was Huitzilopochtli, the Blue Hummingbird in all his magnificence, waving plumes upon his head, stripes upon his face, and Xiuhcoatl, his fire-serpent lightning spear, in his hand.

Brandishing his burning weapon, Huitzilopochtli turned on his sister Coyolxauhqui and hacked her to death, cleaving limb from limb and bone from tendon. Her severed head, her sundered arms, her decapitated torso, her lopped legs, her feet, her hands, her fingers, her toes, all bounced and bobbed and tumbled and rolled down the slope of Coatepec, like bits of a broken doll.

Huitzilopochtli, his task unfinished, then turned on his brothers, the Four Hundred Southerners. Slashing and slicing to right and left, he chased them to the south and slew the upstarts just as the triumphant Sun of dawn slays the hosts of night. In their death, they were transformed into stars.

The day on which Huitzilopochtli proclaimed his supremacy, when the solar god of war was reborn to vanquish the lunar goddess and turn his brothers to stars, has never been forgotten. The name of the day is 1 Flint, in the year 2 Acatl.

After this victory, the Hummingbird again led his people south, to Chalpultepec, which lay in a valley on the shores of a lake. Here they met some old enemies, people of their own kind – the tribes who had chosen to worship Malinalxochitl and from whom they had parted so long ago. Confrontation, not reconciliation, was in the hearts of these rediscovered brothers, under their leader Copil, the son of the Hummingbird's sister. In the battle that followed, Copil and his followers were victorious. He himself, however, was taken by Huitzilopochtli in sacrifice. Cutting out his palpitating heart, the Hummingbird flung it on to a rock in the lake. There the heart swelled and grew and became an island that lay in the middle of the water.

Leaving the scene of battle, the people travelled further, to Culhuacan, on the lake's far shore. Was this, they wondered, their promised land at last, the hoped-for home for which they had searched, foot-slogging it across the wide world, for so many generations? No, it was not. The place where they were forced to settle was the most desolate of wastes, an expanse of lifeless, solidified lava that stretched further than the eye could see or the mind imagine. Here they spent their days in servitude to the Toltec lords, who were its rulers.

And yet against all the odds they thrived, as Huitzilopochtli saw only too well.

'Hmm,' he pondered. 'They like this life too much.' And he instigated a plan that would sow a little discord and advance the fortunes of his people. He told the Aztec leaders that they should ask the Culhua, the inhabitants of Culhuacan, to supply them with a bride, a noble princess of their own blood.

The Culhua, conscious of the Aztecs' warlike nature, complied and, when the princess was duly delivered, the recipients – as was their custom with victims – promptly flayed her and a priest donned her skin. Arrived at the celebrations, the Culhua were horrified to see the grinning priest parading in the bleeding skin of their own princess. Fear gave way to fury and they fell upon the Aztecs, killing many. Others escaped by diving into the lake and swimming across to the island that lay in the middle, which had once been Copil's heart.

And there, as the bedraggled band crawled ashore, what sight met their amazed eyes? Quietly pecking on the flesh of a nopal cactus, a golden eagle sat. An eagle on a cactus on an island in a lake. They had found their promised land.

The Aztecs dammed and channelled the saltwater lake, and created islands and hanging gardens in the swamp, and a great city grew there, the capital of a mighty empire. It was called Tenochtítlan, the Place of the Nopal Cactus Rock.

At Tenochtítlan the Aztecs honoured Huitzilopochtli and built a temple to him, later called the Templo Mayor. The north side belonged to Tlaloc, the god of rain. But the south side was the Hummingbird's and here, under the gaze of his wooden effigy, the priests re-enacted his victory at Coatepec, removing the hearts of their sacrificial victims and tumbling their bodies down the temple steps, just as Coyolxauqui had once fallen at Serpent Mountain.

Founded in the Year of Our Lord 1345, Tenochtítlan has survived. Churches and shops and office blocks now overlay its pagan stones; crowds and cars jostle in its streets; telephones and televisions and a million music-machines disturb its peace; aeroplanes thunder through its skies. But underneath an Aztec heart beats.

Tenochtítlan still lives to this day. It is called Mexico City.

THE FIRST FRUITS

• AZTEC •

IT WAS WITH PRIDE THAT the gods looked on their latest creation – the first human beings, made from fish, blood and bone. But divine approbation is not enough alone to sustain life, as the gods well knew. If these humans were to thrive and multiply, they needed food to fill their bellies, so the gods set out to look for some. Nowhere did they find so much as a berry or a root.

Among the gods was Quetzalcoatl, the Plumed Serpent. It was he who first spotted something which might be useful – a tiny red ant, which was carrying in its jaws a single grain of maize.

'Sister Ant,' he began, 'please tell me – where did you find that wonderful food? Is there more like it? Please show me where it is hidden.'

'Show you where it's hidden?' jeered the ant. 'Do you think I'm completely stupid? If I showed you, you'd take it all and there'd be nothing left for me. It's my secret and I'll not share it with you.'

But Quetzalcoatl persisted and, after much cajoling the ant finally agreed.

'You'd better turn yourself into something smaller,' she said. 'You'll never get into where I'm going decked out in all that frippery you choose to wear – quetzal feathers and rattlesnake scales and baubles and bangles and goodness knows what else!'

So the Plumed Serpent changed himself into something very small and very humble: became a little black ant. He followed his disgruntled guide where she led him, through a tiny crevice into the dark belly of a mountain called Tonacatepetl, the Mountain of Sustenance. It was well named for, deep in its stone heart, a cavernous chamber opened out, which was filled with seeds and grains of every kind. There were kernels of maize and the flat seeds of squash; there were cacao pods whose seeds yielded chocolate; there were beans and the fiery seeds of the pepper and the pips of the tomato. The place was a treasure trove of the seeds of plant life.

Seizing a few maize kernels in his powerful little mandibles, Quetzalcoatl made off, back to where the others were waiting. The gods chewed the kernels to a pulp and then, like mother birds feeding their young, placed the pulp in the mouths of the hungry humans.

One helping of corn mash, however, was not enough to sustain an entire race. For that, all the seeds of Tonacatepetl would be needed. So Quetzalcoatl – back to his old self again – threw a rope over the mountain and tried to carry it away. But Tonacatepetl refused to move.

The gods explained their difficulty to the Grandfather and Grandmother, Oxomoco and Cipactonal. 'How can we obtain the seeds in the mountain?' they asked.

The ancient diviners cast lots to find the answer. 'Nanahuatzin must open the rock,' the wise ones replied.

Now this Nanahuatzin, who would later metamorphose into the glorious Sun, was at this time the lowliest and sickliest of all the gods, and an unlikely choice for such an important task. But the augurs did not lie: if they had spoken his name, then he it must be.

Nanahuatzin set off for the mountain. With him went the blue, white, yellow and red Tlaloque, the rain gods of the four directions and servants of the great Tlaloc. With lightning bolts and other divine devices, the gods split Tonacatepetl open … and out poured the contents of the rock, so long stored up inside. At once the Tlaloque gathered them up – all the seeds and the kernels and the pips and the beans – and carried them away to the four corners of the earth. There they scattered them and fed them with life-giving rain to make them germinate and shoot and in their turn bear seed, so that people would for ever be able to grow their own crops.

That is how the gods gave food to humankind. And when you yourself next eat – fiery chilli, perhaps, or some rich, dark chocolate or a tasty tomato or a cob of butter-glazed corn – remember who first blessed you with these things … and be thankful.

HOW TORTOISE GOT HIS SHELL

• MIXTEC •

Long, long ago, in Oaxaca, a great rain fell. It fell for so long that it drowned everyone and everything.

When the rain stopped and the water dried up, the land was like a big mud bath. In a small corner of the land a little lump of mud began to quiver and take shape. The shape stood up. It was a tortoise, with a shell as smooth as a newly laid egg.

Tortoise looked around him at the extraordinary landscape into which he had been born. Everywhere, on all sides, there were the bodies of those who had drowned in the flood. And feasting on them was the vulture.

It was a horrible scene. Tortoise did not want to stay there. He wanted to be up in the clean blue air, in the drifting clouds, where he could look on the face of God. But without wings to carry him, this was an impossible dream.

He approached the vulture. 'You have wings and you can fly. Fly me to heaven to meet the Maker of Life.'

Vulture ignored him. He was having far too good a meal, gorging himself on dead flesh.

'Fly me to heaven to meet the Maker of Life,' Tortoise persisted. Still Vulture ignored him.

But Tortoise's character was like his gait – slow and steady and resolute. He refused to take no for an answer.

'Fly me to heaven to meet the Maker of Life,' he repeated for the third time.

Vulture was beginning to feel irritated. All he wanted was to be left in peace to enjoy his food in a civilized way. All he got was nag, nag, nag from

this funny-looking creature with his scrawny neck and his bandy legs and his shell as smooth as a newly laid egg. 'Oh, all right then!' he agreed at last, if only to gain a brief respite from his tormentor's querulous voice.

Tortoise climbed on to Vulture's back. He was going to have his wish: he would look on the face of God. Vulture spread his great wings and they took off, soaring up into the boundless blue of the sky. Pressed close against his body, Tortoise took a deep breath – and breathed in Vulture's smell. It was rank. As an eater of carrion, the big bird stank of putrid flesh.

'Ugh!' cried Tortoise, gagging. 'You smell disgusting!'

Vulture paid no attention, but flew higher and higher.

'Aah! I think I'm going to be sick!' Tortoise pulled in his head so as not to breathe in the bird's odour, but it seeped like a creeping infection through all the little openings into his shell.

'You stink. You reek. You smell like excrement!'

Vulture's patience snapped. With a shake of his mighty wings he threw off his talkative passenger, who went tumbling, tumbling, twisting and twirling all the way down through the boundless blue of the sky until he landed on the ground. *Crash!* *Crack!* The impact of his fall broke his shell – until now as smooth as a newly laid egg – into numerous pieces.

The Maker of Life took pity on Tortoise. He mended his shell, patching it together as best he could. But it was never the same again. Tortoise wears it still, a mish-mash of assorted segments of different shapes and sizes. And when he remembers how perfect it once was, he tucks himself inside it to hide his embarrassment.

That is why the tortoise has a patched-up shell. *Verdad verdadero*, my tale is done.

HOW ARMADILLO GOT HIS SHELL

• INCA •

ONE DAY, A BIG PARTY – a fiesta – was to take place at Lake Titicaca. All the animals were going. 'I must look my best,' said Armadillo, and he began to weave a new coat for himself. He could see it perfectly in his mind's eye. It was of such wondrous complexity, such a marvel of the stitcher's art, that all who saw it would be struck dumb with awe. Where did you get that coat? How did you do it? they would say.

Armadillo started at the neck. He intertwined the yarn, slotting woof into warp. The pattern he wove was a lattice of tiny whorls and spirals, as intricate as lace. It was a labour of love – and of time, for such work cannot be accomplished in minutes. But the result, creeping into life on his loom, was truly a wonder to behold.

'Good-day, Brother Armadillo,' said the fox. 'And what are you doing?'

'Go away, Brother Fox. I'm busy.'

'What are you weaving?' the fox persisted.

'Well, if you must know, I'm making myself a new coat for the party at Titicaca.'

'You'd better hurry, then! The party is tonight.'

Tonight? Armadillo was alarmed. It could not be true! He must have got the dates wrong. He could never finish his coat of wonders by tonight … nor could he go naked to the fiesta. In a panic, he began to work faster and more carelessly. *Clickety clack, clickety clack* … the loom rattled and clanked as he slammed the shuttle furiously back and forth. He forgot all his thoughts of artistry, all his dreams about making a grand entrance. He just had to get the job finished.

At last the weaving was done, just in time. But the coat was not what Armadillo set out to create. The little overlapping scales around the head and neck, produced when he had the luxury of time, were small and neat and tight. The plates further down on the back, executed in a hurry, were loose and irregular and messy.

Armadillo put on his new coat and went to the fiesta at Lake Titicaca. The other animals were not, as he had hoped, awestruck. Indeed, some even laughed at him. To hide his shame, he went to ground after this, living in a burrow beneath the earth and only coming out at night when it is too dark to be seen.

The coat that Armadillo made is the only one he has. Like it or not, he has been wearing it ever since. The thread is run, this tale is done.

BAT AND THE RAINBOW

• MIXTEC •

OF ALL THE CREATURES IN the world, Bat was the ugliest and he knew it. He took his grievance to the Master of Life.

'I need feathers to keep off the cold,' he lied. 'S-s-see how I shiver.'

What Bat really wanted were feathers to cloak his drab brown body so that he, too, could dazzle like the birds of rainforest, sierra and plain. But there were no spare feathers to be had: they had all been shared out long ago.

The Master of Life thought awhile. Then he hit upon a compromise: each bird would give Bat a single feather.

No sooner said than done. The air was thick with the flutter of wings as all the birds in creation flocked from the mountains and the uplands and the marshes and the deserts to obey the command of the Master of Life. The hummingbird gave Bat a quill of iridescent violet, the toucan one of sapphire blue. The parrot gave a plume of emerald, the quetzal one of golden-green. The flycatcher, flamingo and ibis gave feathers that burned bright like coral and fire, the eagle, falcon and antshrike ones that glowed silver, indigo and grey. Coverts and crests and pinions and panaches and down quickly mounted in a great fluffy pile like the stuffing from a giant's mattress.

Bat put the feathers on. He felt like a prince – he looked like a prince! In his glorious finery, he reflected light and colour on to everything around him.

'I am beautiful!' he thought to himself. 'No one will despise me now.'

And it was true. The birds were so amazed by him that they lost, temporarily, the power of song.

Bat took to the air. Buoyed by euphoria and the uplift of his multi-layered feathers, he became an aerial acrobat. He cruised the thermals. He dived, he swooped, he plummeted, he soared, he hovered, he looped the loop, he circled, he spiralled, he skimmed the crests of the clouds. And as he performed these aeronautical tricks, he left a trail of colour behind him that cascaded in a vast, sweeping arc across the heavens.

What the people below saw, as they gazed up in awe at the luminous, storm-washed sky, was the first rainbow.

It was then that Bat became vain.

'Who are you …' he said to the iridescent hummingbird, to the jewel-bright quetzal, to the lustrous parrot, '… who are you compared with me?'

It was the same with the other birds. Bat paraded his superiority before them all.

The birds took their grievance to the Master of Life. 'Bat thinks he is better than we are,' they said.

The Master of Life thought awhile, but kept his thoughts to himself.

Bat set off as before to perform his usual aerial display. High in the sky, he proudly shook his beautiful feathers … and, as he did so, they fell from him in tufts and fluttered down to earth like a shower of coloured snow.

Bat was bald and naked.

Quickly he dived for cover. He has not come out since. He hides in caves by day and only comes out at night, flying very fast so that he may not be seen, all the while looking, looking, looking for his lost feathers.

He has never found them. But after a storm, when the Sun illuminates the wet sky, the mark they left may still be seen in the crescent of colour we call the rainbow. The rainbow is Bat's memorial and reminds us that once he, too, had his hour of glory.

WAITING FOR THE DEAD

• YAUYOS •

IN THE PROVINCE OF Huarochirí it was the custom, among the ordinary people, to honour the dead with a wake five days after they had died. Food would be specially prepared and *chicha* placed next to it, to drink. Then all the village would gather to wait. At last, the dead one would return to eat the food, take some *chicha* and say a last goodbye, and then – the rite of passage completed – go to join the ancestors.

But, as time went on, the population grew and the food they produced was hardly enough to go around among the living, let alone feed the dead. And yet still the old custom continued.

Then one day, in a particular village, a man died. All the women got together to make the food for the wake. On the fifth day everything was ready.

They sat down and waited. Noon came. No unearthly footsteps stirred the dust of the sleepy street.

They waited. The Sun began to set. No long, blue shadow announced its owner, rising from the grave.

They waited. The Moon rose, a big silver coin in a cobalt sky. No ghostly presence appeared to set their spines a-tingling.

The guest of honour didn't come.

So everyone gave up waiting and went home to bed. In the darkness, the dead man's wife looked at all the food so carefully prepared and laid out, now a cold and sorry reminder of the party that never was. What a waste! Then she went to bed, too.

In the morning, her dead husband strolled in. 'Anything to eat?' he said.

The woman was beside herself with anger. 'You – you – how dare you show your face now! Don't you know that we waited all day for you and you didn't come? Don't you know how foolish you made me look? You were always late when you were living and you're still late now you're dead!'

The ghost seemed puzzled. 'I'm here now, aren't I … so what's the problem?' he said.

All his wife's self-control snapped. She picked up whatever she could lay her hands on – corn cobs, potatoes, kitchen utensils, stools – and hurled them at her dead husband, who vanished in a puff of vapour and was never seen in the village again.

And it is a curious but well-known fact – news of his experience having spread through the community of spirits and discouraged others newly arrived – that from that day on the dead never again returned from the grave to take food from the mouths of the living.

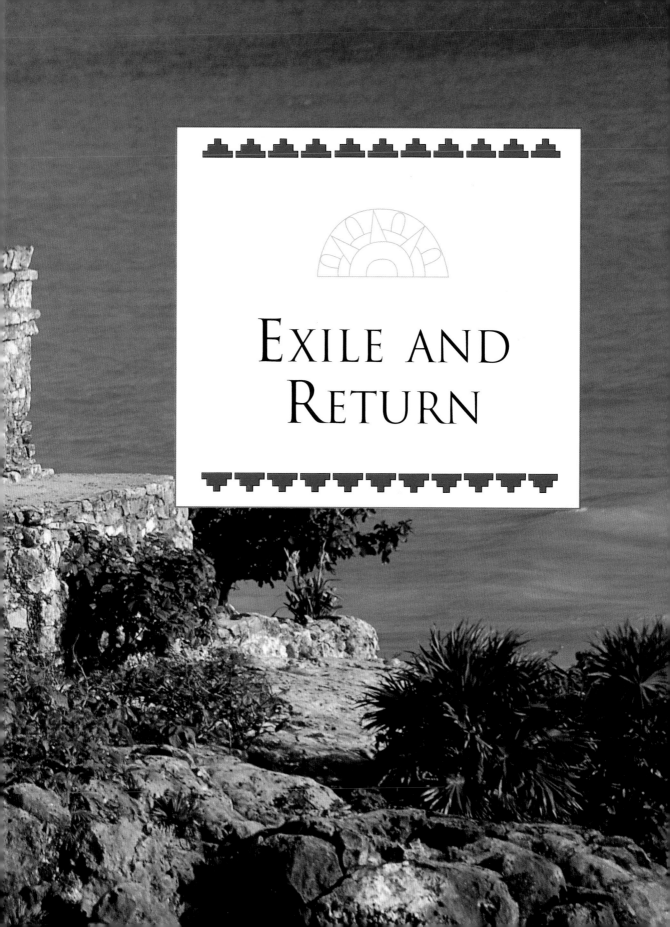

EXILE AND RETURN

THE DEAD AND REBORN saviour god is one of the great themes of mythology and religion. It is an archetype which finds expression in many different cultures, from the risen Christ of the Christian faith and other resurrected gods of the Near East to the Celtic folk heroes Arthur and Fionn Macumhaill, who are not dead but waiting to rise again when their people have need of them. The three legends here, from the Maya, Aztec and Inca traditions, feature similar figures, and are made more poignant by the circumstances in which they are set – the defeat and the near-destruction of these peoples and their cultures by the Spanish invaders.

'The Return of the Morning Star' tells of the exile and anticipated return of the god Quetzalcoatl, the Plumed Serpent, who is forced into exile by the treachery of the dark god Tezcatlipoca. Metaphorically, his expulsion represents the Aztec conquest of the old Toltec heartland. The Aztecs' victory, however, is uneasy, for the year when Quetzalcoatl will return coincides with the appearance of the *conquistadors*, whom the Aztecs mistake for Quetzalcoatl and his party. As the prophecy foretold, the newcomers overthrow the Aztec order, but in a way which is far more devastating and long-lasting than they could have imagined.

The legend of Inkarrí tells a similar tale of reversion. The hero's name is a fusion of 'Inca' and *rey*, the Spanish word for 'king'. The decapitation of certain Inca leaders may have given rise to the image of his severed head. Although buried, the head remains vital, for it is gradually regenerating its lost body and limbs. When this growth process is complete, Inkarrí will – like Arthur and Fionn – rise from the grave to throw off the yoke of the invaders.

The final story, 'The Living', is a particularly beautiful portrayal of the ancient concept of immanence – of a sacred indwelling presence in all of nature. 'The Living' provides a fitting and positive ending to this collection of myths, for it shows how, despite centuries of suppression, a people can still retain a connection to their roots – how, despite the imposition of alien creeds and values, their own sense of wonder and the sacred still inhabits their souls.

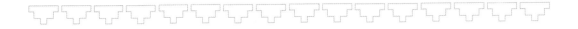

THE RETURN OF THE MORNING STAR

• AZTEC•

'ONE DAY,' said Quetzalcoatl, 'one day I will return. 'And so the people waited for him – the god who had sailed away to the east on a raft of serpents, who was consumed in the blaze of the rising Sun, whose heart became the Morning Star.

For seven hundred years they waited. And they waited with dread in their hearts, for they were the Aztecs, who with the connivance of their god Tezcatlipoca had ousted Quetzalcoatl, stripped him of his power and his possessions, banished him from his beloved Tula and sent him away into exile. Now they were masters of a mighty empire. But the god's parting words still lingered in the shadows of their memory, reminding them that he would come to avenge himself; reminding them that they lived on borrowed time. Just when he would come was not certain.
But the priests and astrologers had predicted the year: it would be Ce Acatl, the year called One Reed.

'One day I will return,' promised Quetzalcoatl.

One day he did.

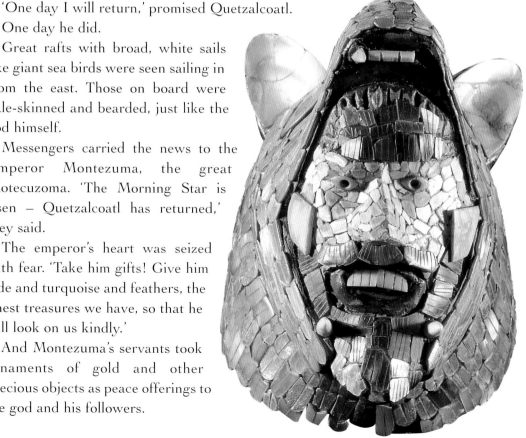

Great rafts with broad, white sails like giant sea birds were seen sailing in from the east. Those on board were pale-skinned and bearded, just like the god himself.

Messengers carried the news to the Emperor Montezuma, the great Motecuzoma. 'The Morning Star is risen – Quetzalcoatl has returned,' they said.

The emperor's heart was seized with fear. 'Take him gifts! Give him jade and turquoise and feathers, the finest treasures we have, so that he will look on us kindly.'

And Montezuma's servants took ornaments of gold and other precious objects as peace offerings to the god and his followers.

But the sight of the gold did not soften the hearts of the strangers, but made them lust for more, for they were not gods but men. Their leader was Hernándo Cortés. The year in which he arrived, as reckoned from the birth date of the alien god whom he worshipped, was 1519. The year, as reckoned on the calendar of the Aztec priests, was Ce Acatl, the year One Reed.

The prophecy had come true.

Montezuma allowed Cortés into Tenochtítlan, his glorious city. Within a year he lay dead, his throat slit, the people say, by a Spanish blade.

Who can master the grief
of Motecuzoma, the sorrows of
Totoquihuatzin

The god who came here
holds heaven and earth
in his hand

The cry of the men
preparing for battle
rides the four winds
A soldier gives birth to the sun

And the chroniclers wrote:
so things fell out in the city of Motecuzoma
called Tenochtitlan, as also in Acolhuacan, city
of Nezahualpilli

With fans of quetzal-bird
feathers the chiefs
returned to their city

Sighs of sadness
fill Tenochtitlan
As the god would have it

HERNÁNDO CORTÉS

Hernándo Cortés (1485–1547) is perhaps the most famous figure in the colonial history of Mexico. Cortés was one of the *conquistadors*, a Spanish word meaning 'conquerors', used to describe those who brought Spanish colonial rule to Central and South America.

Cortés was born into an aristocratic family in the province of Extremadura in Spain. In 1504 he went to live in Santo Domingo in the West Indies, which the Spanish had already started to colonize in the 1490s. In 1517 an expeditionary force brought back reports of large cities in the Yucatán peninsula, then a centre of Maya civilization. In February 1519, against the wishes of the Cuban governor, Diego Velazquez, who distrusted his motives, Cortés led another expedition to Yucatán. With around 650 men and eleven ships, he followed the coast northwards and founded Veracruz, the first Spanish settlement in Mexico. Then, in August of the same year, he marched inland towards Tenochtítlan, the Aztec capital.

Rumours of men in 'iron shirts' (armour) with guns and riding 'deer as high as houses' (horses), which were then unknown in Mesoamerica, filled the hearts of the Aztecs with dread. The timing of Cortés's arrival was ominous because it coincided with the predicted return of the god Quetzalcoatl, which also signalled the ending of the world. In November 1519 the Aztec emperor Montezuma (also known as Moctezuma) allowed Cortés to enter Tenochtítlan and treated him like a god, decorating him with necklaces and garlands and wreathing his head with flowers.

Cortés slowly tightened his hold over Montezuma. Finally he made him a prisoner and ruled the empire through him.

The Aztecs were horrified by the way in which their gifts were treated – artefacts made of gold, for which the Spanish 'lusted like pigs', were melted down, and even more precious featherwork was consigned to the fire. In June 1520 they revolted and hundreds of Spaniards were killed in what became known as *la noche triste* (the sad night). Montezuma also lost his life, but Cortés escaped with the help of the Aztecs' enemies, and spent the next ten months preparing for the siege of Tenochtítlan. By May 1521 the city was surrounded. Weakened by fighting, disease and lack of food, the Aztec army under the new emperor, Cuahtemoc, finally surrendered, after ninety-three days. For the Aztecs, the world had truly ended.

INKARRI

• INCA •

THE SUN IS BORN and the Sun dies, the mighty rise and fall. Such are the cycles of creation, such the ages of humankind.

Atahualpa the Inca lies dead. He died in Cajamarca at the hands of the tall, bearded strangers who came from the sea. The strangers craved gold, that was plain: 'Do they eat it?' Atahualpa said. So great was their lust that even the ransom he gave – a roomful of gold, eighty-eight cubic metres in size, the same twice over of silver – could not save him. The strangers placed a chain around his neck so that he could not escape. They brought him into the square and instructed him in the articles of the Christian faith. And then they cut off his head.

Tupac Amaru the Inca lies dead. He died in Cuzco, led there from his hideaway in Vilcabamba with a golden chain about his neck. Standing on the scaffold in the plaza, he denounced the old gods of his people. And then they cut off his head.

Inkarrí – the Inca *rey*, the king – is not dead but merely sleeping. Who is he, this Inkarrí? He is Manco Capac, the first Inca, the son of the Sun, who threw his golden rod, and where it landed Cuzco was born. He is Atahualpa. He is Tupac Amaru. He is no one Inca and every Inca. All that remains of him is his decapitated head. And slowly, slowly, deep beneath the soil of old Tahuantinsuyu, his head is growing, sprouting a neck and a body and arms and legs. And when at last all the growing is done and he is

FRANCISCO PIZARRO

What Hernando Cortés did for Spanish colonial rule in Mexico, Francisco Pizarro (1478?–1541) did in Peru. Unlike Cortés, however, Pizarro was of humble stock. Born in Trujillo, Spain, he was the illegitimate son of an infantry captain, was raised by his mother's impoverished family, and never learned to read. He left Spain for the West Indies in 1502. In 1509 he took part in a Spanish exploration of the Caribbean coast of Central and South America; in 1513, he was with the expedition that crossed the Isthmus of Panama to the Pacific Ocean, and which led to the founding of Panama City.

Here, Pizarro and the other Spanish inhabitants heard reports of a fabulously wealthy Indian empire somewhere to the south. In 1524, Pizarro, who was now wealthy and powerful, mounted the first of several expeditions down the Pacific coast to find it. After stumbling on the Inca city of Tumbez in modern Ecuador, he returned to Spain to recruit men for a further expedition. In 1531, he and his party of around 170 left Panama City and eventually landed in Ecuador. They marched south, deeper into the Inca empire which, fortunately for them, was in a weakened state due to civil war. At Cajamarca they overcame the Inca ruler Atahualpa in a surprise attack. Despite the vast ransom they received in exchange for his life, they finally executed him in 1533. They advanced to Cuzco, the Inca capital, where they displayed the same level of unabashed greed as the Spanish in Mexico, trampling underfoot the treasures in the Temple of the Sun, pounding them with hammers to make them easier to carry, fighting with each other over their booty, and throwing the golden artefacts into the melting pot to turn them into gold bars.

The Spanish took control of Cuzco later that same year, an event which marked the beginning of the end for the Inca empire. As for Pizarro, governor of Peru and now also a marquis and man of enormous wealth, he was to die at the hands of his own kind. On 26 June 1541, supporters of his former comrade and partner Diego de Almagro, whom he had had garrotted, attacked him, hacking him to death and burying his body in an unknown grave.

whole again, Inkarrí will rise from the grave and banish the conquerors who for so long have oppressed his land. And then he will lead his people once more, into the dawn of a new and glorious age.

The Sun is born and the Sun dies, the mighty rise and fall. Such are the cycles of creation, such the ages of humankind.

We will drink from the skull of the traitor
And from his teeth a necklace make.
Of his bones we will make flutes,
Of his skin a drum.
Then we will dance.

THE LIVING

• MAYA •

Long, long ago, before the *conquistadors* came, the people lived peacefully by the shores of Lake Atitlán. They went quietly about their daily business and they worshipped Heart of Heaven. They were the Tzutuhil Maya.

Now there were some among them who were wise beyond human understanding. These were the shamans, the seers, the *brujos* – witches – and the *naguales*, who could turn themselves into spirits. The power of magic was in their breath and in their blood so that they could, whenever they wished, become invisible and vanish into the air, into the lake, into the mountains or the hills.

But then the time of the *conquistadors* came. Many people were killed. The Tzutuhil met together at the place now called Santiago Atitlán to discuss what they should do.

A shaman and a lord of the people addressed the great crowd gathered there: 'We are many', they said, 'and we could stand and fight, but then much blood would be spilt. There is a better way. We have spoken with Heart of Heaven and this is what we must do. Those who have the power of magic, let them vanish and go where they will go. Others who cannot do this must remain. But there will be no war.'

And so it was agreed. But before the wise ones – the shamans and the seers and the *naguales* and the *brujos* – disappeared, they spoke to those who were staying behind.

'You will never be alone,' they said. 'Even though you cannot see us we will be with you always, in the air and the earth and the rocks and the water. Do not forget us.'

And the people never have. When they leave their houses in the morning, or go into the hills or out on to the lake, they throw a kiss to the air or take a handful of water and kiss it, saying: 'Our mothers, our fathers, our grandmothers, our grandfathers, bless us and be with us in the joys and sorrows of this day and night.'

The ancestors are there still. They are in the whisper of the wind. They are in the voice of the thunder. They are in the gentle touch of the rain. They are in the rustle of the leaves, in the sighing of the trees and in the murmuring water.

Listen. Can you hear them?

'We are not dead,' they say, 'but living.'

GLOSSARY OF NAMES

• AZTEC •

CENTZON HUITZNAHUA – The Four Hundred Southerners, sons of **Coatlicue** and brothers of **Huitzilopochtli**, who transforms them into stars. They recall the Four Hundred Boys who become the Pleiades in Maya myth.

CHALCHIUTLICUE – Lady Precious Green, She of the Jade Skirt. Goddess of lakes and streams, and consort of **Tlaloc**.

COATLICUE – She of the Serpent Skirt. Earth Mother and guardian of Coatepec, Serpent Mountain.

COYOLXAUHQUI – Lady Golden Bells who wears bells on her cheeks. She is the daughter of **Coatlicue** and is associated with the Moon.

EHECATL – see **Quetzalcoatl**.

HUITZILOPOCHTLI – Solar deity and war god, patron god of the Aztecs. His birth from the head of **Coatlicue** suggests his subordination of her cult.

MAYAHUEL – Goddess of the maguey plant, from which alcoholic *pulque* is made.

MICTLANTECUHTLI – God of Death and Mictlan, the Underworld, which he rules with his wife Mictecacihuatl.

NANAHUATZIN – The sickly god who, through self-sacrifice on a pyre, becomes **Tonatiuh**, the Sun of the Fifth Age of creation.

OMETEOTL – 'Two-God', a bisexual creator who embodies the notion of duality. The deity's male aspect is Ometecuhtli and female aspect Omecihuatl.

QUETZALCOATL – From *quetzal*, a species of bird, and *coatl*, a rattlesnake, he is the Plumed Serpent Toltec god adopted by the Aztecs (see also **Tezcatlipoca**). He is associated with Venus as Morning Star (see also **Xolotl**). As Ehecatl, he is the Wind, the 'roadsweeper' god who clears the way for the rain.

TECUCIZTECATL – Sun god who becomes the Moon when a rabbit is thrown in his face.

TEZCATLIPOCA – The Smoking Mirror, god of shadows and sorcery who carries a black obsidian mirror of a type used for divinition. Paired with the 'light' **Quetzalcoatl**, he is the 'dark' half of a duality, a form prevalent in Mesoamerican thought.

TLALOC – God of Rain and Lightning.

TLALTECUHTLI – Female sea monster, often a cayman, from whose body **Quetzalcoatl** and **Tezcatlipoca** make Earth and Sky, a classic method of creation.

TLAZOLTEOTL – Goddess of Purification, particularly of sexual vices. She eats *tlazolli*, filth or excrement, and is therefore a type of Sin-Eater or Scapegoat.

TLAHUIZCALPANTECUHTLI – Lord of the Dawn and god of the Morning Star. As Itztlacoliuhqui (or Ixquimilli), he is god of coldness and of stone.

TONATIUH – Sun God. See also **Nanahuatzin**.

XIPE TOTEC – The Flayed God, deity of Spring rejuvenation and patron of goldsmiths. The flayed human skin he wears suggests new growth arising from the husk of the old.

XLOTL – Canine god and *alter ego* to **Quetzalcoatl**. Associated with Venus as the baleful Evening Star.

XOCHIQUETZAL – Flower Quetzal, the goddess of erotic love and the arts. Her flower is the marigold.

• INCA •

CONIRAYA – A creator deity also known as Coniraya Viracocha, from Huarochirí, east of Lima.

HUAYALLO CARHUINCHO – Volcano god and the chief deity of the Huarachirí region.

INTI – Sun God and brother-husband to **Mama Quilla**.

MAMA QUILLA – Moon Goddess and sister-wife to **Inti**.

PACHACAMAC – Coastal creator deity, sometimes identified with **Viracocha**.

PARIACACA – Mountain god and victorious opponent of **Huayallo Carhuincho**, suggesting the replacement of one cult of worship by another.

VIRACOCHA – Highland creator deity, also known as Con Ticci Viracocha.

• MAYA •

CHAC – God of Rain and Lightning.

GUCUMATZ – The Plumed Serpent, the Quiché Maya equivalent of the Aztecs' **Quetzalcoatl**.

HUNAHPU – One of the Hero Twins, brother to **Xbalanque**, and son and nephew of the divine twins Hun Hunahpu and Vucub Hunahpu. He becomes the Sun.

HURACAN – Hurricane, Heart of Heaven, creator deity and storm god. As a Triple God, he has three aspects embodying three forms of thunderbolt.

ITZAMNA – Aged creator god and husband to **Ixchel**.

IXCHEL – Aged goddess of midwifery and healing, and wife to **Itzamna**.

KUKULCAN – The Plumed Serpent god of the Maya of Yucatán. (See also **Gucumatz**.)

TOHIL – Patron god of the Quiché Maya.

VUCUB CAQUIX – Seven Macaw, defeated by **Hunahpu** and **Xbalanque** and transformed into the Big Dipper.

XBALANQUE – One of the Hero Twins, brother to **Hunahpu** and son and nephew of the divine twins Hun Hunahpu and Vucub Hunahpu. He becomes the Moon (probably the full Moon).

XMUCANE – Divine Grandmother and Midwife, Diviner and wife to **Xpiyacoc**. As Crone, she may also represent the waning Moon.

XKIK – Blood Moon, princess of Xibalba, the Underworld, and mother to **Hunahpu** and **Xbalanque**. As Maiden, she may represent the waxing Moon.

XPIYACOC – Divine Grandfather and Diviner, husband to **Xmucane**.

INDEX

PICTURE CREDITS

All photographs by Mireille Vautier, Paris.

Page 2 Temple of Quetzalcoatl (detail).
Culture: Teotihuacan, 200–600 CE. Teotihuacan, Mexico.
Page 3 Jade mask representing King Pacal.
Culture: Maya classic, 600–700 CE. Palenque, Chiapas, Mexico.
National Museum of Anthropology of Mexico City.
Pages 4–5 Hand-woven textile, 'tocapu', with Inca designs.
Culture: Inca, 1400 BCE – 1532 CE. National Museum of
Anthropology and Archaeology of Lima, Peru.
Page 8 Detail of a 'manto' (textile made of cotton); each mythic
personage is holding a trophy-head. Culture: Paracas Necropolis,
1000–500 BCE. National Museum of Anthropology and
Archaeology of Lima, Peru.
Page 9 Laminated gold necklace representing a half-moon.
Culture: Frias, 100 BCE – 700 CE. Brüning Museum,
Lambayeque, Peru.
Page 10 Jade representing three high-ranking personages, found
in the sacred cenote of Chichen Itzá. Culture: Maya, post-classic,
1000–1500 CE. Museum of Merida, Yucatan.
Page 12 Stone head. Culture: Maya classic, 700–800 CE.
Ruins of Copan, Honduras.
Page 13 The feathered serpent, Kukulcan. Culture: Maya
post-classic, 1000–1200 CE. Temple of Venus, Chichen Itzá,
Yucatan, Mexico.
Page 14 The Florentine codex: Human sacrifice.
Culture: Aztec dates of the codex: 1571–1573 CE.
Antochiw Collection, Mexico.
Page 16 Inca accounting system: 'quipu'. Culture: Inca,
1400–1532 CE. National Museum of Anthropology and
Archaeology of Lima, Peru.
Page 17 Stone stela covered in glyphs. Culture: Maya classic,
700–800 CE. Ruins of Copan, Honduras.
Page 18 Florentine codex. Cortés is presented a feathered head-
piece by Montezuma's envoys. Culture: Aztec. Dates of the codex:
1571–1573 CE. Mexico City General Archive.
Page 19 Borbonicus codex. The god Chalchiutotoli.
Culture: Aztec. Dates of the codex: probably 1519–1540 CE.
Mexico City National Library.
Pages 20–21 Lake Titicaca, border of Peru and Bolivia
in the Andes.
Page 23 Laminated gold idol representing a woman with a
deformed head. Culture: Frias, 100 BCE – 700 CE.
Brüning Museum, Lambayeque, Peru.
Page 24 Wooden mask with shell eyes. Culture: Chancay,
1100–1500 CE. National Museum of Anthropology and
Archaeology of Lima, Peru.
Page 25 Sacsayhuaman ruins. Culture: Inca, 1400–1532 CE.
Cuzco, Peru.
Page 26 Detail of gold pectoral representing a personage wearing
a head piece. Culture: Lambayeque, 1200–1400 CE.
Brüning Museum, Lambayeque, Peru.
Page 27 Terracotta representing a woman offering a child.
Culture: Bahia, 700–800 CE. Central Bank Museum,
Quito, Ecuador.

Page 28 Ceramic representing a hunter. At the bottom, a trophy-
head. Culture: Nazca, 200 BCE – 500 CE. National Museum of
Anthropology and Archaeology of Lima, Peru.
Page 30 Magliabecchiano codex. The god Quetzalcoatl.
Culture: Aztec. Date of codex: before 1566 CE.
Mexico City National Library.
Page 31 Magliabecchiano codex. The god Mictecacihuatl ('Feast
of the Dead'). Culture: Aztec. Date of codex: before 1566 CE.
Mexico City National Library.
Page 33 Magliabecchiano codex. Mictlantecuhtli, the god of the
Dead. Culture: Aztec. Date of codex: before 1566 CE.
Mexico City National Library.
Page 34 Volcanic stone representing a 'Cihuateteo'.
Culture: Aztec, 1350–1521 CE. National Museum of
Anthropology of Mexico City.
Page 36 'Tumi': gold ceremonial knife representing the god
Nyam Lap. Culture: Chimu, 1100–1500 CE. Museum of Gold,
Lima, Peru.
Page 37 'Pyramid of the Magician'. Culture: Maya classic,
900–1150 CE. Uxmal, Yucatan, Mexico.
Page 39 The god Kukulcan, the feathered serpent. Culture: Maya
post-classic, 1000–1200 CE. Temple of Venus, Chichen Itzá,
Yucatan, Mexico.
Page 41 Stone calendar Culture: Aztec, 1350–1521 CE.
National Museum of Anthropology of Mexico City.
Page 42 Wool offerings to the dead representing women. Culture:
Chancay, 1100–1500 CE. Amano Museum, Lima, Peru.
Page 43 Troano codex: sculptor of glyphs. Culture: Maya,
date unknown. Antochiw Collection, Mexico.
Page 45 Magliabecchiano codex.
Culture: Aztec. Date of the codex: before 1566 CE.
Page 46 Magliabecchiano codex. The god Chicomexochitl (seven
flowers). Culture: Aztec. Date of the codex: before 1566 CE.
Mexico City National Library.
Pages 48–49 El Castillo, also called the Kukulcan Pyramid.
Culture: Maya post classic, 1000–1200 CE.
Chichen Itzá, Yucatan, Mexico.
Page 51 Magliabecchiano codex: auto-sacrifice through the
tongue. Culture: Aztec. Date of the codex: before 1566 CE.
Mexico City National Library.
Page 52 (top and below) Borbonicus codex: the gods
Tlatocaocclotl and Tlatocaxolotl carry flags.
Culture: Axtec. Dates of the codex: c. 1519–1540 CE.
Mexico City National Library.
Page 54 Florentine codex, the god Quetzalcoatl.
Culture: Aztec. Dates of the codex: 1571–1573 CE.
Antochiw Collection, Mexico.
Page 55 Funerary mask covered with turquoise and coral.
Culture: Teotihuacan, 200–600 CE.
National Museum of Anthropology of New Mexico.
Page 56 Borbonicus codex, the god Pantecatl, god of pulque.
Culture: Aztec. Dates of codex: c. 1519–1540 CE.
Mexico City National Library.
Page 57 Funerary mask made of laminated gold.
Culture: Lambayeque, 1200–1400 CE. National Museum of

Anthropology and Archaeology of Lima, Peru.
Page 59 Troano codex, the 'red' god and the god Itzamna represented as 'Atlantes'. Culture: Maya, date unknown. Antochiw Collection.
Page 61 Sculptured jade representing a serpent, found in the sacred cenote of Chichen Itzá. Culture: Maya post-classic, 1000–1500 CE. Museum of Merida, Yucatan, Mexico.
Page 62 Painted bottle representing the god Tlaloc. Culture: Toltec, early post-classic, 950–1200 CE. National Museum of Anthropology of Mexico City.
Page 63 Detail of a painting, Maya Sea-Coast Village. Culture: Maya post classic. Carnegie Institution by Morris & Charlot, 1931 (date of the document).
Page 65 Jade pendant representing a man wearing a 'maxtlatl'. Culture: Maya post-classic, 1000–1200 CE. Chichen Itzá, Yucatan, Mexico.
Page 67 Detail from the ballcourt. Culture: Maya post-classic, 1000–1200 CE. Chichen Itzá, Yucatan, Mexico.
Page 68 Cospiano codex, representation of an owl. Culture: Aztec. Date of codex: post-conquest. Mexico City National Library.
Page 69 Detail of a Tzompantli. Culture: Maya post-classic, 1000–1200 CE. Chichen Itzá, Yucatan, Mexico.
Page 70 Troano codex, painted in black, the god 'M' holding a spear and prisoner with his hands attached. Culture: Maya, date unknown. Antochiw Collection, Mexico.
Page 72 Stone glyph. Culture: Maya classic, 600–700 CE. Palenque, Chiapas, Mexico.
Page 73 Ceramic containing original maize. Culture: Inca, 1400–1532 CE. National Museum of Anthropology and Archaeology of Lima, Peru.
Page 74 Ballcourt scene. Culture: Cotzumalhuapa, 600 CE. Hacienda Las Ilusiones, Guatemala.
Page 76 Vaticanus codex: Ocomatli, the ape. Culture: Aztec, date unknown. Mexico City National Library.
Page 78 Tracano codex, a rabbit. Culture: Maya, date unknown. Antochiw Collection, Mexico.
Page 79 Magliabecchiano codex, the ballgame. Culture: Aztec, date of codex: before 1566 CE. Mexico City National Library.
Page 80 Ceramic representing an owl. Culture: Mohica, 100 BCE – 700 CE.
Pages 82 and 83 Troano codex where two gods 'M' wearing pagnes are sitting face to face. Culture: Maya, date unknown. Antochiw Collection, Mexico.
Page 84 Painting representing a raided village and a procession of victors and captives. Culture: Maya post-classic. Carnegie Institution by Morris and Charlot, 1931 (date of the document).
Page 85 Vaticanus codex, rabbit from the legend of the moon and the rabbit. Culture: Aztec, date unknown. Mexico City National Library.
Page 87 Florentine codex, human sacrifice. Culture: Aztec. Dates of the codex: 1571–1573 CE. Mexico City General Archive.
Page 88 Troano codex, the god of merchants beats the sky with an axe to obtain rain. Culture: Maya, date unknown. Antochiw Collection, Mexico.
Page 89 Borbonicus codex, tzompantli with the skull. Culture: Aztec. Dates of codex: c. 1519–1540 CE. Mexico City National Library.
Page 91 Temple of the inscriptions. Culture: Maya classic, 600–700 CE. Tula, Mexico.
Page 92 Volcanic stone representing Quetzacoatl. Culture: Toltec, 950–1200 CE.
Page 94 Troano codex, Ek Chuah, the god of merchants presenting an offering in the shape of the glyph Kan, a reference to maize. Culture: Maya, date unknown. Antochiw Collection, Mexico.
Page 96 Inca jar called 'aribalo'. Culture: Inca, 1400–1532 CE. National Museum of Anthropology and Archaeology of Lima, Peru.
Pages 98–99 The city of Machu Picchu in the high forest. Culture: Inca, 1400–1532 CE. Cuzco Province, Peru.

Page 101 Borbonicus codex, Mayahuel, the goddess of maguey. Culture: Aztec. Dates of codex: c. 1519–1540 CE. Mexico City National Library.
Page 103 (top) Borbonicus codex, detail from a sacrifice related to the sun and moon. Culture: Aztec. Dates of the codex: c. 1519–1540 CE. Mexico City National Library.
Page 103 (below) Magliabecchiano codex, tiger skin buried with the merchant. Culture: Aztec. Date of codex: before 1566 CE. Mexico City National Library.
Page 104 16th-century manuscript made of amatl paper representing 'Tochtli' the rabbit. Culture: Aztec. Mexico National Archive.
Page 105 Ceramic representing a bird. Culture: Nazca, 200 BCE – 500 CE. Amano Museum, Lima, Peru.
Page 107 Mythical creature on El Dragon Temple. Culture: Chimu, 1100–1500 CE. Trujillo, Peru.
Page 108 Funerary gold mask with lapis lazuli eyes from Sipan tomb. Culture: Mochica, 100 BCE – 700 CE. Brüning Museum, Lambayeque, Peru.
Page 109 The living quarters in Machu Picchu. Culture: Inca, 1400–1532 CE. Cuzco Province, Peru.
Page 110 Stone monolith. Culture: Tiahuanaco, 400–1400 CE. Bolivia.
Page 112 Painting representing the son of the Sun, Manco Capac, founder of the Inca Empire, Cuzco School, anonymous, 18th century. Pedro de Osma Museum, Lima, Peru.
Page 113 Painting on a sacred wood vase called 'Kero' representing a symbolic agriculture ceremony where seeds are made of gold. Culture: Inca, 1400–1532 CE. Arteaga Collection, Yucay, Peru.
Page 114 Detail of the Temple of the 100 Columns. Culture: Maya post-classic, 1000–1200 CE. Chichen Itzá, Yucatan, Mexico.
Page 116 (top and below) Troano codex. Two representations of the same god, the god 'F'. One is wearing a type of parrot as a head piece, the other has an eagle on his head. Culture: Maya, date unknown. Antochiw Collection, Mexico.
Page 117 Stone statue of an animal. Culture: Cotzumalhuapa, 600 CE. Hacienda 'las Ilusiones', Guatemala.
Page 119 Terracotta in the shape of a personage used to carry incense. He represents the god of maize. Culture: Maya post-classic, 1000–1500 CE. Museum of Merida, Yucatan, Mexico.
Page 121 Viracocha on the Gate of the Sun. Culture: Tiahuanaco, 400–1400 CE. Bolivia.
Page 122 Gold llama: idol used as an offering. Culture: Inca, 1400–1532 CE. National Museum of Anthropology and Archaeology, Lima, Peru.
Page 124 Agricultural terraces in Machu-Picchu. Culture: Inac, 1400–1532 CE. Cuzco Province, Peru.
Page 126 Kaolin ceramic representing a wild cat with its body shaped like a snake. Culture: Pashash, 300 BCE – 600 CE, Ancash province. National Museum of Anthropology and Archaeology, Lima, Peru.
Page 127 Borbonicus codex, eagle. Culture: Aztec. Dates of codex: c. 1519–1540 CE. Mexico City National Library.
Page 129 Boturini codex representing the Aztec migration toward Tenochtitlan. Culture: Aztec. Dates of codex: 1530–1540 CE. Mexico City National Library.
Page 131 Aztec warrior wearing the feathers of the sacred bird, the Quetzal. Culture: Aztec. Painting from a codex by Salvador Melo (contemporary artist). Private Collection, Mexico.
Page 133 Duran codex representing the legend of the foundation of Tenochtitlan: an eagle standing on a nopal is eating a serpent. Culture: Aztec. Dates of codex: 1579–1581 CE. Antochiw Collection, Mexico.
Page 134 Magliabecchiano codex representing 'Tlaloc', God of the rain, associated with maize. Culture: Aztec. Date of the codex: before 1566 CE. Mexico City National Library
Page 136 Terracotta representing a tortoise with the head of an

anthropomorphic figure carrying an offering. Culture: Maya post-classic, 1000–1500 CE. Museum of Merida, Yucatan.
Page 138 Coca bag made of gold representing a wild cat. Culture: Mochica, 100 bce – 700 CE. Museum of Gold, Lima, Peru.
Page 141 Sacsayhuaman ruins. Culture: Inca, 1400–1532 CE. Cuzco, Peru.
Pages 142–143 One of the temples of Tulum on the Carribbean Sea noticed by the Spanish sailors before the conquest. Culture: Maya post-classic, 1500 CE. Quintana Roo, Mexico.
Page 145 Bearded personage, covered with shells, in the mouth of an animal. Culture: Toltec post-classic, 950–1200 CE.
Page 147 Hernándo Cortés. Antochiw Collection.
Page 148 The conquest of Peru, note at the top the Sun, 'Inti', God of the Incas. Culture: Inca colonial.
Collection Chavez Ballon, Cuzco, Peru.
Page 149 The conquest of Mexico, the Spaniards helped by the Tlaxcaltecs on the road to Tenochtitlan. Culture: Tlaxcaltec. Anonymous, from the Lienzo of Tlaxcala.

Page 150 Fragment of terracotta in the shape of a personage used to carry incense. Culture: Maya post-classic, 1000–1500 CE. Museum of Merida, Mexico.
Endpapers Cospiano codex representing a calendar. Culture: Aztec. Date of codex: post-conquest.
Mexico City National Library.
COVER
Background: Hand-woven textile, 'tocapu', with Inca designs. Culture: Inca, 1400 BCE – 1532 CE. National Museum of Anthropology and Archaeology of Lima, Peru.
Details from: the Cospiano codex, the Vaticanus codex, and the Borbonicus codex.

Acknowledgements
The photographer would like to thank: Dr Hermilio Rosas, Dr and Mrs Walter Alba and Mrs Amano from Peru, Pr. Michel Antochiw and archaeologist Agustin Pena Castillo from Mexico for their invaluable help with her work.

ACKNOWLEDGEMENTS

Poem Credits
The poems quoted in the text are taken from the following sources:
page 26 – quoted in Ninian Smart, *The World's Religions*, 2nd edition
(Cambridge University Press, 1998), page 183.
page 29 – quoted in W. S. Merwin, *Technicians of the Sacred*, ed. Jerome Rothenberg
(Anchor Books, New York, 1969), page 237.
page 44 – from *Popul Vuh*, trans. Dennis Tedlock
(Simon & Schuster, 1996), p.147.
page 97 – from Garcilaso de la Vega, *The Royal Commentaries of the Inca*, trans. Maria Jolas, ed. Alain Gheerbent (Orion Press, New York, 1961), pages 81–82, quoted in Merwin, *Technicians of the Sacred*, page 240.
page 125 – from Eduardo Galeano, *Memory of Fire: 1. Genesis*, trans. Cedric Belfrage (Random House, New York, 1985), p.173. Translation © Cedric Belfrage. Reprinted by permission of Pantheon Books, a division of Random House, Inc.

page 146 – quoted in Merwin, *Technicians of the Sacred*, page 226.
page 150 – from Eduardo Galeano, *Memory of Fire: 1. Genesis*, page 107.

The author wishes to acknowledge the invaluable reference provided by Dennis Tedlock's outstanding translation of the *Popul Vuh*, published by Simon & Schuster in 1996.

The publisher has made every effort to contact the copyright holders of the poems quoted in this book and would welcome any information regarding omissions.

Publisher's Acknowledgements
With grateful thanks to Julian Baker, Liz Cowen, Ingrid Lock, Juliet Standing and Mireille Vautier for their help.